Britney Crosby
Age: 12

Description: Brown hair, brown eyes. Last seen wearing a red and yellow sundress in the Black Lagoon Water Park.

This message brought to you by the Monster Police.

www.EnterHorrorLand.com

HorrorLand

MISSING

ESCAPE HORRORLAND

Britney Crosby
Age: 12

Description: Brown hair, brown eyes. Last seen wearing a red and yellow sundress in the Black Lagoon Water Park.

This message brought to you by the Monster Police.

www.EnterHorrorLand.com

HorrorLand

MONSTER BLOOD FOR BREAKFAST!

Goosebumps HorrorLand™

ALL-NEW! ALL-TERRIFYING!

1. REVENGE OF THE LIVING DUMMY
2. CREEP FROM THE DEEP
3. MONSTER BLOOD FOR BREAKFAST!
4. THE SCREAM OF THE HAUNTED MASK
5. DR MANIAC VS ROBBIE SCHWARTZ

Goosebumps®

NOW WITH BONUS FEATURES!

NIGHT OF THE LIVING DUMMY

DEEP TROUBLE

MONSTER BLOOD

THE HAUNTED MASK

ONE DAY AT HORRORLAND

MONSTER BLOOD FOR BREAKFAST!

R.L. STINE

SCHOLASTIC

Scholastic Children's Books
An imprint of Scholastic Ltd
Euston House, 24 Eversholt Street
London, NW1 1DB, UK
Registered office: Westfield Road, Southam, Warwickshire, CV47 0RA

First published in the US in 2008 by Scholastic Inc.
This edition published in the UK by Scholastic Ltd, 2008
Goosebumps series created by Parachute Press, Inc.

ISBN 978 1407 10691 5

British Library Cataloguing-in-Publication Data.
A CIP catalogue record for this book is available from the
British Library

Printed and bound by CPI Group (UK) Ltd, Croydon, CR0 4YY
Papers used by Scholastic Children's Books are made from
wood grown in sustainable forests.

16

www.scholastic.co.uk/zone

3 RIDES IN 1!

MONSTER BLOOD FOR BREAKFAST!

1

My name is Matt Daniels, and my terrifying story began on a typical morning. In my house, *typical* means *totally annoying*. Because who showed up just as my sister, Livvy, and I were finishing our breakfast?

The kid from next door. Bradley Wormser.

Everyone at school calls him Worm, and it's a pretty good nickname for him. Trust me.

Bradley shows up in our kitchen almost every morning, just as Livvy and I are finishing breakfast. And he gobbles up whatever he can grab.

He's so skinny, it's hard to believe he could eat everything on the kitchen table if we let him. He really does look like a long, lanky worm with glasses!

I have this idea that one day I'm going to *glue* the Pop Tarts to the table. Then I'm going to enjoy the look on Bradley's face as he struggles to pull them up.

I'm great at inventing stuff. And I'm really interested in science. And I'm a pretty good athlete.

But none of that helps me against Worm Wormser. He drives me nuts!

This morning, Bradley waited till my mom's back was turned. Then he dropped a fat, dead horsefly into my cereal. I stared down at the fly floating on top of the milk.

"Yucko," Bradley said. "You don't want that, do you, Matt? There's a dead fly in it."

He pulled the bowl away from me, tilted it to his face, and drank the cereal down. Then he spat the fly on to the floor. "Not bad," he said, using Livvy's sleeve to wipe his mouth. "A little soggy."

"Let go of me!" Livvy cried.

He snapped his fingers a centimetre from her nose. He thinks that's totally funny. Livvy hates it.

Mom has no idea what a pain Bradley is.

She was cleaning something at the sink. "Mom, can I have another bowl of cereal?" I asked.

"No seconds, Matt," she replied without turning around. "You've got to watch your weight. Your big swim meet is coming up soon, remember?"

My stomach growled. Angrily, I grabbed a wet glob of cornflakes from Livvy's bowl with my fingers – and stuck it on to Bradley's nose.

Mom turned around. "Matt!" she shouted, glaring at me. "Don't play with your food!"

"Yeah, Matt. Don't play with your food," Bradley said, grinning.

As soon as Mom went back to cleaning, he made a grab for Livvy's Pop Tart.

Mom turned around again just as Livvy snatched it away. "Livvy, no fighting!" she snapped.

"But, Mom—"

See what I told you? You spell Bradley's name P-A-I-N.

This was the most important week of my life. And I didn't need Bradley in my face.

I would love to invent something to make the creep disappear. Or maybe I could just *ask* him to disappear. But there are a few problems.

For one thing, he lives in the house right next door. And his mom and my mom are business partners. They both run a party catering business from our homes.

This means that Livvy, Bradley and I are thrown together a lot.

And there's one other big problem. Bradley *worships* me.

This morning, Bradley put his paws all over my new swim team T-shirt. "Matt, can I have this shirt? Where'd you get it? It's awesome. It's kinda small on you – isn't it?"

He always wants to dress like me. He thinks it will make him popular, too. It's pitiful, right?

And the guy never stops talking. "Did you see that scary movie on HBO last night? *Claw*? It totally creeped me out. When those two claws reached out of the basement and grabbed the kid by the shoulders?"

He squeezed Livvy's shoulders with both hands. "Just like this. Ha-ha! I'm the vicious CLAW!"

"Stop! Let *go*!" my sister screamed.

"Livvy," Mom scolded. "Stop being such a crab."

Bradley laughed. He waited till my mom left the kitchen. Then he pulled a small orange-and-black can from his backpack. "Matt, check this out. Go ahead. Open the lid. I dare you."

I groaned. "Now what?"

Worm spends all his time online. He plays these sci-fi battle games till late at night. And he's always sending away for all kinds of weird things.

He shoved the can towards me. "Go ahead. Open it," he said.

I pushed his hand back. "No way."

He grinned. "OK. I'll do it."

He gripped the lid and started to turn it. Then, suddenly, he stopped, and his eyes went wide. His smile faded. "Watch OUT!" he screamed. "It's gonna BLOW!"

The lid popped off and clattered to the floor. I stared into the can. Empty.

Bradley laughed.

And then I smelled something. Something heavy and damp and rotten floating up from inside the can. Like dead fish, only much worse. Like year-old *spoiled milk*.

"Ohhhh." I grabbed my stomach and let out a groan. I tried to hold my breath.

Too late. The sick smell invaded my nose. And now I could *taste it* on my tongue!

"Ulllp!" My stomach lurched. I started to gag.

I jumped to my feet and ran to the bathroom. Livvy was retching loudly. She came running right behind me, her hand pressed tightly over her mouth.

I could hear Bradley laughing his head off. He has a hee-haw donkey laugh. Obnoxious.

Leaning on the bathroom sink, I took several deep breaths. My stomach heaved. I couldn't get the pukey smell from my nose and mouth. And I could smell it on my clothes. I glanced at the clock. No time to change. I was going to smell like sour milk at school all day!

I trudged back into the kitchen. Bradley was still laughing at his stupid joke. "That was a riot!" he said. "You both turned green! Ha-ha!"

He held up the empty can. "Check it out."

In big black letters, the label read: **GAS ATTACK. A PARTY FAVOURITE!**

Livvy had tears in her eyes. Her hands were balled into tight fists. I knew she wanted to murder Bradley. So did I. But what could we do?

"You guys totally *stink*!" he said. And he laughed his hee-haw donkey laugh some more.

What could be more embarrassing than walking to school with Bradley every morning? Livvy took off and ran, her red ponytail flying over her backpack. "So long, suckers!" she shouted.

I was stuck with him. No way to escape.

It's only three streets away to Shandy Hills Middle School. But with Worm beside me, it always seems like three *kilometres*.

"I have those same trainers," Bradley told me. He stomped down hard on my foot. "But mine aren't scuffed up like that," he said.

"Give me a break," I muttered.

He ran ahead a few steps, then pushed a hand against my chest to stop me. Then he opened his backpack and fumbled around inside it.

"Swear you won't tell anyone about this," he whispered. "I've got something here I bought online that will totally impress Mr Scotto."

"No way," I said, jumping away from him. "If it's another stink can, keep it to yourself!"

"No. This is serious," he said. He swatted a fly off his stringy brown hair. Then he pulled a tiny jar from his backpack. "This is no joke. This is a big deal."

A school bus rumbled past and turned on to Willis Street. I glanced around. We were the only kids in sight. "Bradley, we're going to be late," I said.

I *hate* to be late. I'm a competitive swimmer, remember. I like to be *first* – not last!

Bradley spun the lid off the tiny glass jar. Inside, I saw a jagged piece of white rock.

"Know what it is?" Bradley asked. His brown eyes flashed. "Don't try to guess. It's a piece of rock from the planet Venus."

"Huh?" I cried. "Are you kidding me? Bradley, how could you fall for such a stupid—"

"*You're* stupid, Matt!" he shouted. "It's real. One of our space probes brought it back. There are only ten rocks like this on earth. And I won an auction for it. Would you believe it only cost me twenty dollars?"

I just shook my head. I didn't know what to say. Bradley and I are both twelve years old. Old enough to know you can't buy a rock from Venus for twenty dollars.

He pulled it out of the jar and placed it carefully in my hand. "Is this going to score points with Mr Scotto or not?" he asked. "Don't be too jealous, Matt. But this could win me the Science Prize."

The Science Prize was a big deal. I'd been working on my project for weeks.

Mr Scotto is our maths and science teacher. But he's also a celebrity in Shandy Hills.

He used to be an astronaut. This year, he started a contest in our school. He said he'd award five hundred dollars and a free month at NASA Space Camp in Florida to the kid in his class who created the most original science project.

Cool, right?

And since I'm the science freak in school, everyone expects me to come up with something great. And I think I have a really good idea. But how could I compete with a rock from the planet Venus? This couldn't be real, could it?

I turned the rock over in my hand and studied it carefully. It was solid white, kinda chalky, and very cool to the touch.

"Whoa, wait!" I held it up close to my face. I struggled to read the tiny type engraved in the stone.

"What's your problem?" Bradley said. "Give it back."

"Bradley, bad news," I said. "Didn't you read the tiny type?"

He blinked. "Tiny type?"

I nodded. "Yeah. It says 'made in China'."

"Not funny!" he cried. "You are *so* not funny."

He grabbed the stone out of my hand. He raised it close to his face. And froze.

I wasn't kidding him. It really *did* say MADE IN CHINA on it.

Bradley shrugged. "No biggie," he said.

Bradley says that a hundred times a day. "No biggie . . . no biggie. . ."

Totally obnoxious, right?

"No biggie." Bradley pulled back his arm – and *heaved* the stone at the stop sign on the corner.

It made a *ping* sound as it hit the metal sign. Then I froze in horror as the stone bounced off – and flew into the windshield of a passing car.

It happened so quickly. The *crack* of the windshield. The shattering *tinkle* of glass as it caved in. The *squeal* of brakes.

Through the broken glass, I saw the angry scowl on the driver's face.

Bradley moaned. "I don't *believe* it! I was aiming at the stop sign."

He saw the driver staring at us. Bradley pointed at me. Then he shouted as loud as he could, "Why did you throw that stone, Matt?"

Bradley took off, running down the street.

Too late for me to run. The driver's door swung open. He pulled himself out of the car.

And I let out a low moan as I saw who it was – our teacher, Mr Scotto.

Later at lunch, I didn't feel much like eating. I put some kind of sandwich on my tray and an apple. I forgot to pick up a drink. I was still in a daze, I guess.

I carried my tray across the canteen to the table where my buddies from the swim team sat. I slumped down into a chair with a loud sigh.

"Matt, what's your problem?" Kenny Waters asked. He crushed a soda can in his hand and tossed it at a group of girls at the next table. They cried out angrily and called him some ugly names.

"I had a little *thing* with Mr Scotto this morning," I murmured.

"No way!" Kenny replied. "You're his star. No way he's going to pick on you."

"He didn't exactly pick on me," I said. I didn't feel like talking about it. I was trying to erase it from my mind. But it wasn't easy.

When Mr Scotto came storming out of his car, I

took the rap for Bradley. I didn't snitch on him. No one likes a snitch, right?

Mr Scotto is big and tall and athletic. He works out all the time. He's got biceps a foot high. I mean, you don't really want to get on his bad side.

He looks like the astronauts you see on TV. Very short, flat haircut; broad, tanned forehead; and blue eyes that seem to stare right through you like lasers.

Well, he was definitely aiming lasers at me this morning.

"I'm really sorry," I told him, shaking my head. "It was a total accident. The stone slipped from my hand and bounced off the stop sign and. . ."

I'm pretty good at talking my way out of trouble. But Mr Scotto was very angry. He said the car was only a month old.

He knows I'm not a bad kid. I think he believed it was an accident.

"My insurance will probably cover it," he said. "If not, I'll have to call your mom and dad about it."

I sighed. It was my own fault. Maybe I *should* have snitched on Bradley. Mr Scotto's warning about calling my parents repeated and repeated in my head all morning. Each time I thought about it, I got angrier.

Bradley really is *a worm,* I told myself. *I've* got *to do something about him.*

I had this idea for a new invention. It was called

Bradley in a Can. When you twisted off the lid, a bunch of disgusting brown worms came flying out.

The idea made me laugh.

Suddenly, I felt an elbow poke into my side. "Yes or no?" Kenny asked.

I stared blankly at him.

He laughed. "You really are on Mars today!" he said. "We were talking about the swim meet championship this week."

"You ready?" Jake Deane asked. "Are you taking the extra practices with the coach?"

Huh? Extra practices? "Well . . . for sure," I said.

The bell rang. I jumped to my feet and picked up my tray. I hadn't eaten a thing.

I've gotta get over this, I decided. *I have to stop being angry at Bradley and concentrate all my energy on the swim team.*

Forget about Bradley. . . Forget about Bradley. . . Forget about Bradley. . .

The next day, I took my seat in Mr Scotto's maths class and tossed my backpack to the floor. Of course Bradley sits next to me. Where else? He's my shadow!

He tapped me on the shoulder. "Yo. What's up?"

I shook his hand off my shoulder and stared straight ahead. I just ignored him. Maybe he'd take the hint.

We had a maths test. Twenty algebra equations to solve.

They were pretty easy. I'm good in maths. Equations are like doing puzzles, and I like solving puzzles.

I leaned over the test page, my pencil filling in answers. Next to me, I kept hearing Bradley's chair squeak. I glanced at him quickly.

Would you believe it? The Worm was staring at my answers, then writing them down.

I glanced back again. I wasn't imagining it. Bradley was definitely copying from me.

Did Mr Scotto notice?

I raised my eyes to the front of the room. No. The teacher was leaning over his desk, reading a book. He kept looking up at the clock. We had only ten minutes left.

Whew. I felt a little relieved. He didn't see Bradley cheating.

But then I felt Bradley's breath on my neck. And Bradley whispered, "Don't go so fast."

Too loud.

Some kids turned around.

I froze. The pencil fell from my hand.

Mr Scotto jumped to his feet. "What's going on?" he boomed. He narrowed his eyes on Bradley and me. "Are you two comparing answers?"

"Matt, you don't have to keep showing me your answers," Bradley said, loud enough for the whole room to hear. "I can do the test on my own."

4

My heart skipped a beat.

I couldn't take the blame for Bradley again.

Cheating was serious in our school. I knew I could be suspended for this. And then what about the swim meet? My teammates were all counting on me. It was the championship – the biggest meet of my life.

And what would Mom and Dad say if I was forced to miss it?

How could Bradley *do* this to me?

"Matt, Bradley, put down your pencils," Mr Scotto said. "I need to talk to you both." He waved us to the front of the room.

I could barely breathe. I didn't believe this was happening.

"No biggie," Bradley whispered, following me to the front of the room. "He loves you. You can talk us out of this."

Mr Scotto rubbed a hand over his short hair. He eyed us both, shaking his head. "I do not allow cheaters in my class," he said sharply. "I'd like you both to go stand in the hall till the test is over. You both get zeros."

"But – but—" I sputtered. "It's not my fault. I didn't *do* anything. It was Bradley. He—"

Mr Scotto raised a hand to silence me. "Not another word," he said. "You know how I feel about taking responsibility."

He wouldn't listen to me. "Are you . . . going to suspend us?" I asked in a trembling voice.

"I haven't decided," he replied.

I glared furiously at Bradley. He stood there with a stupid grin on his face.

Bradley will probably say "No biggie" when we get out in the hall, I thought. *And I'll have no choice. I'll have to punch his lights out. And then I really* will *be suspended – for good. And then I'll have to punch his lights out* again.

Mr Scotto held the classroom door open. Still grinning, Bradley stepped out into the hall.

I started through the door. Mr Scotto followed me. "Listen, Matt," he whispered. "It's nice of you to try to help Bradley. But don't take it too far."

I stared at him.

"You don't have to cheat to help him," Mr Scotto continued. "This is Strike Two, Matt. I don't understand what's got into you. I know you must be tense about the swim meet. But one more strike, and I'll have no choice. I'll have to suspend you from school."

"But, Mr Scotto, I—"

He closed the classroom door behind me. I glanced up and down the hall. Empty. I heard voices and laughter from the next classroom.

Bradley leaned against a locker. I stomped over to him and grabbed him by the front of his T-shirt. "Why did you do it?" I growled. "Why did you copy my answers?"

He still had that sick grin on his face. "You're the maths king, right?" he said. "Who *else* am I going to copy?"

After school, I picked up Livvy from Shandy Hills Elementary, and we walked home. She began kidding around – bumping me with her backpack, trying to trip me. Livvy is eight. She thinks that stuff is funny.

But I was in no mood. I started walking faster to get away from her.

"I heard you got in trouble today," she called.

"Huh?" I swung around and stared at her. "How did *you* hear about it? You're not even in the same school."

"Some kids were talking," she said.

Oh, great. The big news was spreading all over town. Perfect Honour Roll student Matt Daniels is a big cheater.

Thank you, Bradley.

I lowered my head and started to cross the street. Mr Scotto's words echoed in my mind: *This is Strike Two, Matt. . . But one more strike, and I'll have no choice. I'll have to suspend you from school.*

Mom wasn't home, so I used my key. I climbed the stairs and opened the door to my room. "Oh, no!" I moaned. "What are YOU doing here?"

Bradley sat in front of my laptop. He kept typing for a bit, then spun around. "Your computer is faster than mine," he said. "You don't mind if I use it – do you?"

A growl escaped my throat. I realized my hands were balled into tight fists.

"Also, I borrowed this T-shirt from your dresser. Mine got a stain on it," Bradley said. "It looks better on me, don't you think? OK if I keep it?"

The tie-dyed shirt said PEACE, LOVE, ROCK & ROLL FOR EVER on the front. It belonged to my dad. He gave it to me last Christmas. It's my favourite shirt.

I stepped up behind Bradley and wrapped my hands around his neck. "Should I kill you now or wait till after dinner?" I said.

He grinned at me. He thought I was joking. "What's your problem, Matt?" he said.

I backed away. I'm not a violent dude. I couldn't let Bradley turn me into one. "Hel-lo! You got me in a *mess* of trouble today," I said.

He shrugged his skinny shoulders. "No biggie," he said.

"Huh?" I couldn't help it. I reached for his neck again. But he rolled out of my reach on the desk chair.

"You're Mr Scotto's pet," Bradley said. "He thinks you're a future astronaut or rocket scientist or something. You know he won't do anything to you."

"But – but—" I was so angry, I started to sputter. "Do you know how important this week is to me? You're *dead meat* if you ruin it for me. I mean it!"

Bradley began snooping through the papers on my desk. He picked up a red notebook. "Are these the plans for your science project?" he asked. "What is it? Some kind of birdhouse?"

I grabbed the notebook out of his hand. "Yeah. If you really want to know," I said. "It's a birdhouse with a computer chip in it."

He giggled. "A computer chip in a birdhouse? Weird!"

"It's not weird," I said. "The chip controls the lights and the air temperature inside. And it controls an automatic seed feeder."

Bradley thought about it for a moment. "Way cool," he said. "You're gonna be a great scientist. Maybe if I stick close enough I will, too."

Yuck-o. Give me a *break*.

He stood up and gave me a salute. Then he walked out of my room and clomped down the stairs. I let out a sigh of relief when I heard the front door close behind him.

"Good riddance," I muttered. He really gets my stomach churning.

I knew I had to calm down. So I filled my big yellow watering can with water. And I carefully watered my ivy plants.

I have two of them in clay pots next to my dresser. Their shiny leaves trickle down the wall, almost to the floor.

I spend a lot of time watering them, and cleaning their leaves, and fixing their soil. Here's a secret. . . Sometimes I even *talk* to them.

Caring for my two ivy plants always calms me down. They started out as a science project. I wanted to see how they grew under different amounts of light. But now I just like to have them and take care of them.

I watered them carefully. Then I straightened some of the leaves. Turning back to my desk, I glimpsed my laptop. What did Bradley leave on the screen?

I studied the monitor. Two bloodshot eyes stared back at me. And under them, in big green letters, the words MONSTER BLOOD.

What is *Monster Blood*? One of Bradley's weird online games?

I looked for an X in the upper right corner to get rid of it. No X.

I hit the ESCAPE key.

The eyes still stared out at me. The words MONSTER BLOOD oozed down the screen like thick clots of green slime.

I hit the DELETE key again and again. I tried several other keys.

I couldn't exit. No matter what I tried, the ugly bloodshot eyes stared out.

And then I heard a scratchy whispered voice, low at first and then louder: "Enjoy your *Monster Blood*. . . Enjoy your *Monster Blood*. . . Enjoy your *Monster Blood*. . ."

The cold, raspy voice gave me the creeps.

I pushed the MUTE button on the front of the laptop. Silence now?

No. The whispered words still poured out: "Enjoy your *Monster Blood* . . . Enjoy your *Monster Blood*. . ."

I pushed the MUTE button again. Again.

"Enjoy your *Monster Blood*. . ."

What was going on? Why couldn't I get it to stop?

My heart started to race. What did Bradley do to my computer?

I slammed the laptop closed. Then I waited a minute or two for it to shut down.

When I raised the lid, the eyes stared out at me. Stared out as if they could see me. The words MONSTER BLOOD oozed down the screen. And the voice whispered again and again: "Enjoy your *Monster Blood*. . . Enjoy your *Monster Blood*. . ."

"NOOOOO!" I cried.

I yanked the power cord from the back of the laptop, then I flipped it over. Fumbled with the battery lid. Finally, pulled the battery out.

Breathing hard, I gaped at the screen. The laptop had no power . . . no power of any kind.

But still the red eyes glared out at me. And the raspy voice continued to whisper its message: "Enjoy your *Monster Blood*. . . Enjoy your *Monster Blood*."

"*YAAAIIII!*" I couldn't help it. I let out an angry scream. I slammed the laptop shut again.

Livvy came running in from the bathroom in her bathrobe. She had a towel wrapped around her wet hair. A few shampoo bubbles clung to her forehead.

"Matt – what's wrong?" she cried. "Are you hurt?"

"Bradley!" I shouted. I shook my fists in the air.

Her blue eyes went wide. She knows I'm always the calm one in the family. I'm the one who's good in emergencies.

There's only one thing in the world that makes me totally lose it. Bradley Wormser.

Livvy wrapped the towel tighter around her wet hair. "What did he do?" she asked.

"Played one of his dumb jokes," I said. "He messed up my computer. Fixed it so it won't turn off."

"Won't turn off? Really? Did you try unplugging it and taking out the battery?" Livvy asked. She's pretty good with computers for an eight-year-old.

"Of *course* I tried that," I snapped. I pushed past her and headed to the door.

"Matt, where are you going?" Livvy called after me.

"To Bradley's," I said.

"Are you going to hurt him? Can I watch?"

I didn't answer. I stomped down the stairs and crossed the garden and walked through Bradley's kitchen door. The kitchen was bright and warm and smelled of cinnamon. Mom and Mrs Wormser must have been baking.

Bradley was standing at the sink, squeezing a yellow cupcake in his hand. He had vanilla frosting smeared around his mouth.

"Sorry I can't share," he said. "This is the last one."

I stared at my tie-dyed shirt. I saw a spot on the pocket. "Give me my shirt!" I shouted. "Now!"

"Whoa." His brown eyes went wide. He shoved the whole cupcake into his mouth and swallowed it without chewing. "What's your problem, Matt? I just *borrowed* it!"

"Give it back!" I demanded. I started across the room towards him.

"OK, OK." He started to pull off the shirt. He was so skinny, I could see all his ribs.

"What did you do to my computer?" I asked. "Did you think that was funny?"

He handed me the shirt. "Excuse me?"

"You messed with my computer," I said. "One of your stupid jokes. You fixed it so I can't turn the thing off."

He shook his head. "No way. You're crazy."

"And you're a liar!" I shouted.

"No way," he repeated. He shoved back his scraggly hair with both hands. "Are you *sick* or something? You're acting like a total nutcase."

I stared at his skinny ribs. "You look like a plucked chicken," I said with a laugh. "Everyone calls you Worm. But they *should* call you Chicken Bones!"

His face turned bright red. "Oh, yeah?" he cried. I could see he was hurt. "You won't be making fun of me very long," he said.

I laughed again.

"You'll see," Bradley said. "I found something awesome. It's going to make me bigger and stronger than even you, Matt. And then you'll talk to me with some *respect*."

"That's tough talk for a pile of chicken bones," I said.

I know, I know. It wasn't very clever. But I was still too angry to think clearly.

I swung around and stomped out the kitchen door. At least I got my dad's shirt back. That made me feel a little better.

Outside, I turned and looked through the window. Bradley was reaching for another cupcake.

When I got home, Mom was sitting at the kitchen table. She had a tall glass of iced tea in her hand.

She glanced at the clock over the sink when I walked in. "Matt, hi. Were you at swim practice?"

"No," I said, rolling the shirt in my hand. "I had to get something back from Bradley."

She mopped her forehead with a paper napkin. "I'm beat. I just got back from next door. Shirley and I baked eight dozen chocolate and vanilla cupcakes today. Can you imagine?"

I sniggered. "Bradley was enjoying a few of them," I said.

Mom groaned. "Shirley and I told him he couldn't have any. They're for a big party on Saturday."

"Face it. He's a creep, Mom," I said.

Mom frowned at me. "Don't say that. He's your friend. You two have known each other your whole lives. And let's be honest. Bradley *knows* he can't compete with you in sports, or in science, or in popularity. So he does these things just to get your attention."

"He's still a creep," I said.

My mobile vibrated. I pulled it out of my jeans pocket. I had a text message from Bradley:

CAN I GET UR SHIRT BACK? FITS ME BETTER.

I worked on my science project till after midnight. The next morning, I woke up a little late. I pulled on my cool new black-and-white Raiders jersey and my jeans and hurried down to breakfast.

Bradley was already at the kitchen table, gobbling down a toasted muffin. He stood up when I came in. “Check it out, dude,” he said. He stretched out his arms.

He was wearing the same Raiders jersey.

“We’re twins!” he said, and slapped me on the back.

Great way to start the day.

“Matt, want some eggs this morning?” Mom asked.

“No time,” I muttered. “I have to go change my shirt.”

Before class began, Mr Scotto called me to the front of the room.

My brain spun. What did I do wrong *this* time? I couldn't think of anything.

Did he want to talk about his broken windshield again?

My heart started to pound as I stepped up to his desk. "Morning," he said softly. He took my arm and led me out into the hall, away from the other kids.

Kids were still at their lockers or making their way to their classrooms. I studied Mr Scotto's face. I couldn't tell whether he was angry or not.

He smelled like peppermint. I think it was his aftershave. He had a small cut on his chin from shaving.

He leaned against the tile wall. "How's it going?" he asked.

I shrugged. "OK, I guess."

He nodded. "I just wanted to say, you're doing a great job with Bradley."

I stared at him. Bradley? What kind of a job did I do with Bradley? I hated his *guts*!

"He told me you helped him think up an idea for his science project. He showed me his plans for his computerized birdhouse. And they are terrific."

I exploded. "His WHAT?!"

"You'll have to work very hard to top him, Matt," Mr Scotto said. "Bradley is definitely the front-runner for the Science Prize. His birdhouse is *brilliant*!"

Oh, no. Please – no.

This was too much. I couldn't talk. I couldn't *think*.

I felt as if my head was about to pop like a balloon. I never felt so angry, so *furious* in my life.

How could Bradley do that to me? Did he really think he could get away with it? Win the prize by stealing my idea?

I squeezed my fists so tight, my fingernails dug into my palms. "Uh . . . Mr Scotto. . .?" I said through gritted teeth. "I have to tell you something about that idea."

He grinned at me. "That was such a nice thing to do for Bradley," he said. "I'm going to forget all about that little cheating thing. I'll let you make up the maths test."

"Uh . . . thanks," I muttered. What could I say? I needed that maths grade. But I couldn't let Bradley get away with stealing my project – could I?

Checking his watch, Mr Scotto walked back into the classroom.

Locker doors slammed. The hall was emptying out.

I tried to calm down. But then I spotted Bradley in the corner, showing off his Raiders jersey to a couple of girls. And I couldn't stop myself.

I hurtled myself at him. Grabbed him hard with both hands. And slammed him against a locker.

He stumbled back, his eyes wide with surprise. His glasses fell off and hit the floor.

Behind me, a crowd had gathered. Where did they all come from?

"FIGHT! FIGHT! FIGHT!" they began to chant.

"FIGHT! FIGHT! FIGHT! FIGHT!" Their voices rang in my ears.

I saw red. I knew I was out of control. But I couldn't help it.

I pressed Bradley against the locker with both hands.

And heard an angry woman's voice from down the hall. *"What's going ON here?"*

Mrs Grant. The principal.

The chanting stopped. The kids behind me didn't move.

Mrs Grant pushed through the crowd. She's a tiny woman, frail and old. She wears grey skirts and grey jumpers. She looks like a sparrow, with short, shiny white hair.

"Stop it! Stop it!" she screamed. She grabbed my arm and pulled me off Bradley.

"Matt, are you fighting?" she asked, still holding my arm.

Oh, no. Oh, no. Oh, no.

I realized instantly that I was in HUGE trouble.

Strike Three. The words flashed into my mind.

Mrs Grant slowly let go of my arm. She stared hard at me with her sharp black sparrow eyes.

Strike Three and you're out, I thought.

Bradley slid to the side, smoothing out the front of his Raiders shirt. His face was very pale. He bent to pick up his glasses.

"You know I have no choice," Mrs Grant said. "The school rules say no fighting of any kind. I have to suspend you, Matt."

"I – I—" I wanted to explain. But what could I say?

Mrs Grant shook her head. "I don't understand," she said softly. "Why would you do this on the day before the swim championship? You know how much our team is counting on you."

This isn't happening, I thought. *This CAN'T be happening to a nice guy like me.*

Mrs Grant pointed down the hall. "Go clean out your locker," she said. "I'm really sorry, Matt. But rules are rules. I'll call your mother right now to let her know. You're suspended from school for a week."

My legs felt weak. My mouth hung open in disbelief. I felt drops of sweat running down my forehead.

"Go," Mrs Grant said, pointing again towards my locker.

Suddenly, Bradley spoke up. "But we weren't fighting!" he said.

Mrs Grant squinted at him.

Bradley hung an arm around my shoulder. "Matt and I are best friends," he told her. "We were just goofing on each other."

The principal frowned. I could tell she didn't believe Bradley.

"It wasn't a fight at all," Bradley said. "We were acting out this scene we saw on TV last night."

"Yeah. That's right," I chimed in. "It was an awesome fight scene. These two guys totally wrecked each other. Bradley and I thought it was funny. We were just pretending to be those crazy guys."

"That's the truth," Bradley lied. He still had his arm around my shoulder like we were best buddies.

I wiped the sweat off my forehead with the back of my hand. My legs still felt shaky and weak.

Was Mrs Grant buying our story? She *had* to – or I was doomed.

She studied us both, rubbing her tiny pointed chin. The hall was silent. I never heard such a deep silence in my life.

"OK," she said finally. "Go back to class, you two." She turned to me. "I didn't think you'd fight in school, Matt. You're too smart for that."

"Th-thanks," I stammered.

She started back towards her office. "No more violent TV shows," she called back. "You guys should watch the National Geographic Channel instead. Keep you out of trouble."

Bradley had a huge grin on his face. His brown eyes were practically *twirling* with excitement. He slapped me a high five.

"Dude, I saved your life," he whispered.

I waited till Mrs Grant turned the corner. Then I gave Bradley an angry shove. "I should *pound* you!" I said.

"Huh?" He backed away.

"You wrecked my laptop with some dumb *Monster Blood* thing!" I screamed. "And after everything else, you stole my science project! I'm warning you. After the swim meet, you'd better *hide*! Because I'll be coming for you!"

"Don't get your boxers in a twist," Bradley replied. "You can keep your dumb birdhouse. I have something new on the way. Something *awesome*. I had it sent overnight. My whole *life* is going to change – big time!"

I laughed. "You'll *still* be a worm!"

"You'll see," Bradley said. "I'll show it to you tonight. You won't be calling me names for long."

Swim practice went on for two hours after school. We had a lot of practice races. Coach Widdoes had tips for us after each race.

The championship meet was the next day. Less than twenty-four hours away!

This was our last chance to tune up.

My three events are the 100-metre freestyle, the 500-metre freestyle, and the 200-metre butterfly. No one can touch me in these races. I always blow everyone out of the water.

But this afternoon, Kenny Waters and Jake Deane tied with me on both events. After the second tie in the butterfly, we were holding on to the pool wall, trying to catch our breath. Shaking off water, they both stared at me in surprise.

Jake laughed. "Did I get faster, or did you slow down?" he asked.

I spat a mouthful of water on him. "I *let* you two tie," I joked. "I just wanted to give you a thrill."

Coach Widdoes leaned over the pool. He's tall and lean, with spiky black hair and the hairiest arms I've ever seen. We all call him Wolf – but not to his face.

"Concentration, Matt," he said to me. He tapped his temple. "It isn't the physical. It's the concentration. Know what I'm saying?"

I nodded. I tapped my temple, too.

Widdoes is a pretty smart guy. I guess he could tell my mind kept slipping to other things. Like this morning. Like coming *so close* to being kicked out of school.

I got changed quickly and began walking home. The sun was already dropping behind the trees. The air grew cool, and deep shadows shifted over the pavement.

I was half a street away from my house when two men stepped out from behind a car and blocked my path. "Hey!" I cried out.

They were both dressed in black trousers and black hoodies. Their hoods were pulled down low over their heads. Their faces were hidden in the evening shadows.

I tried to sidestep them. But they closed in tight on me.

"Don't move, kid," one of them said in a deep, low voice.

"Let me go!" I screamed. "What do you *want*?"

They were both big and solid, built like tree trunks. Their dark eyes glowed from under their black hoods.

A chill ran down my back. I wanted to run. But my legs were shaking so hard, I could barely *stand.* I could see my house. So close . . . so close.

One of them stuck out a big hand. He had jewelled rings on every finger. "No trouble, sonny," he said.

"That's right." His partner spoke up. He stuck out his hand, too. I saw a tattoo of a spider on his palm. "If you just hand it over to us, there won't be any trouble," he said.

I tried to swallow. My mouth was suddenly as dry as cotton. "Huh? Hand *what* over?" I choked out. "Who *are* you?"

"We're your friends," Spider Tattoo replied. "We only want to help you." He glanced behind him, as if to see if anyone was watching.

"But, but—" I sputtered.

"Don't act scared," Ring Fingers snarled. "You ordered it. But we need it back."

I glanced around. Why wasn't there anyone on the street? Anyone who could rescue me?

"Ordered?" I said. My voice came out shrill and high. "I – I didn't order anything."

"Come on, kid," Spider Tattoo said. "Don't make it hard for us. A terrible mistake was made."

"Truth," his partner chimed in. "The stuff is dangerous. I mean, *very* dangerous. No joke. We can't let you keep it." His eyes kept darting all around.

"We never should have sent it," Spider Tattoo said. "We'll get in BIG trouble if anyone finds out."

"Do you have it on you?" his partner asked. "Is it in your backpack there? Just hand it to me, OK? No problem."

"No," I started. "I told you. I don't—"

Ring Fingers pointed towards my house. "You have it at home? You can give it to us there. We'll come with you."

What were they after? What could be so dangerous? Why were they so desperate to get it back?

I didn't know how to answer them. I only knew I didn't have it. "You – you've made a mistake," I stammered. "I—"

Bright white lights rolled over us. I glimpsed the men's faces. Hard. Tough looking.

I turned and saw a green car pull up to the kerb. The passenger window rolled down. Mr Scotto poked his head out. "Matt – how's it going? How was practice?"

I dived to the car and grabbed the door handle. I leaned down close to Mr Scotto. "Those two men," I whispered. "They're really scary. I don't know what they want."

His eyes went wide. He gazed past me. "Men?" he said. "I don't see any men."

I swung around.

They had vanished into thin air.

10

After dinner, I was up in my room, bending over my ivy plants. I was using plant shears to cut them back.

I gasped as I felt cold, hard fingers wrap around my neck. "Hey!"

Livvy laughed. She pulled her hands away.

"Why do you love sneaking up on me like that?" I asked.

She shrugged. "Because it's fun?"

"Get me a rubbish bag for the clippings," I said.

"Like I'm your servant?" She gave me a push and danced away. "Those plants are creeping along the floor," she said. "Like in a horror movie. One night, they're gonna creep into your bed and strangle you."

Livvy has a good imagination.

"If they get really long, they'll reach to *your* room," I said.

I heard loud thuds on the stairs. A few seconds later, Bradley came bursting into the room. "My two favourite people!" he exclaimed.

"Bye," Livvy said, rolling her eyes. She hurried out as fast as she could.

Bradley strode up to me, an excited grin on his face. He was wearing baggy khakis and my Shandy Hills swim team sweatshirt. I never gave it to him. He must have stolen it from my closet.

"Check this out, dude," he said breathlessly. I could smell spaghetti sauce on his breath. I tried to back away, but he had me cornered.

He held up a small green plastic egg. "I already took it out of the box. I couldn't wait. This is gonna change everything," he said. He was so excited, his hands were trembling as he held up the egg.

"I ordered this online from a secret site," he said. "I am so *psyched*!"

I gazed at the plastic egg. The same size as a real egg. "What kind of secret site?" I asked.

"You can't get on it unless you know *three* secret passwords," Bradley said.

He waved the green egg in front of my face. "Know what this stuff does?" he asked.

"Makes an omelette?" I joked.

"It grows," Bradley said. "Once you open the egg, it grows and grows. And if you EAT it, you grow, too. Bigger and stronger."

I rolled my eyes. "Hel-lo. Bradley, you are a total sucker. You really believe the stuff in this egg will make you grow? How can you be so dumb? How could you fall for another fake?"

"No. No," Bradley said, breathing hard. "No way this is a fake. This stuff is for real, Matt. Know what I'm going to do?"

I shrugged. "I can't guess."

Bradley rolled the plastic egg in his hand. "I'm gonna eat just a tiny chunk," he said. "Just enough to make me gain weight and grow big muscles. Then I won't be a skinny worm any more."

I laughed. "Give me a break," I said. "I can't believe you're serious."

"I'm totally serious," Bradley said. "After I eat this, I'll be a different person. I'll be strong. And athletic. I won't have to copy you. I'll be *better* than you!"

"But, Bradley—"

"Kids will invite me to parties. And choose me to be on their football teams. And want to hang out with me," Bradley went on. "And you'll stay home by yourself talking to your ivy plants."

"Let me see it," I said.

He dropped the egg into my palm. It was warm and damp from his sweaty hand.

I raised it close to read the words engraved in the green plastic: **MONSTER BLOOD**.

"Whoa. Wait," I said. Suddenly, it all came clear to me. "Bradley, did you send for this last night when you were using my laptop?"

Bradley nodded. "Yeah. So?"

The two men in black flashed into my mind. I pictured their hard faces, their dark, angry eyes.

This Monster Blood had to be what they were after.

Bradley ordered it on *my* computer. So they think I have it.

And they're desperate to get it back. Because . . . because it's so *dangerous*!

I stared at the innocent little egg. I used to have Silly Putty that came in an egg like this.

So . . . why were those two men so eager to get it back?

What's *wrong* with this stuff?

The plastic egg suddenly felt hot in my hand. . .

11

I set the Monster Blood egg down on my desk.

"Give it to me," Bradley said. "I'm not going to wait. I'm going to take a taste right now. I'm serious. This is going to change my life."

He shoved my shoulder. "And guess what, dude? This Monster Blood is going to win me Mr Scotto's Science Prize, too. Know what the Science Experiment is? ME!"

Bradley did a wild dance around my room, tossing his arms in the air and cheering for himself.

I had a heavy feeling in my stomach. I gazed at the green egg. "Bradley, I have to tell you about these two men," I started. "They—"

Bradley stopped his crazy dance. "Don't try to talk me out of it," he said. "My mind is made up, Matt. This is the biggest thing I've ever done, and I know it's going to be awesome."

"But, Bradley, let me tell you—" I tried again.

"No. No way," he said. He clamped a hand over my mouth to silence me. "I'm going to eat just enough Monster Blood to make me as big and strong as you. Read my lips. No one will ever call me Worm again."

I pulled his hand off my face.

I should stop him, I told myself. *Those two men in black said this stuff was really dangerous. Bradley is a creep. But I can't let him eat something that might make him ill.*

Yes, Bradley is a creep. A creep...

Suddenly, my mind returned to the past few days. All the close calls. Mr Scotto's broken windshield. Bradley getting us caught cheating on the maths test... My wrecked laptop... Almost being suspended from school...

All because of Bradley.

A creep. A total creep.

I couldn't help it. My anger came sweeping back. It flooded over me. *Payback time,* I told myself.

Bradley deserves it.

I grabbed the egg off my desk. I pulled off the top. And gazed at the bubbling green gook inside.

Then I raised the Monster Blood to Bradley. "Go ahead," I said. "Slurp it up."

Bradley's face turned serious as he took the egg from me. He held it in one hand and raised it close to his face.

"It's bubbling a lot," he murmured. "Ha-ha. Listen. Hear that *plop plop* sound? Weird? Let's see what it tastes like."

He dipped his little finger into the green goo.

"Hey, it's hot," he said. "And real sticky. Look how it sticks to my finger."

"Go crazy," I said. "Taste it."

"Say goodbye to the old Bradley," he said. And he lifted his little finger to his mouth.

12

Bradley stuck out his tongue. He raised the little glob of Monster Blood to his mouth.

And I grabbed his arm and pulled it down. "No!" I cried.

"What are you *doing*?" Bradley said angrily. "Let go. What's your problem, Matt?"

He tried to lift the Monster Blood to his mouth, but I held his arm away. "I can't let you do it," I said.

I changed my mind. I guess I have a conscience. I couldn't do something that evil – even to Bradley.

"Let GO of me!" Bradley screamed. "You're not the *boss* of me!"

That made me laugh. "Big baby!" I said. I grabbed his little finger and wiped the glob of Monster Blood off on his jeans. Then I grabbed the bottom part of the egg and clamped the top down on top of it.

I had to squeeze the lid on. The Monster Blood was rising up out of the egg.

"Give it to me!" Bradley swiped at the egg. But I swung it out of his reach. "It's *mine.* I can do what I want with it," he whined.

"Just shut up and listen to me," I said. "Two men stopped me on the street. They said it was dangerous. They wanted it back."

Bradley rolled his eyes. "Two men? Ha-ha," he said. "Tell me another one."

"I'm *serious*," I said. "I can't let you eat this stuff."

"You're a dirty liar!" Bradley shouted. He dived at me, grabbing for the plastic egg. I raised it out of his reach.

He tackled me to the floor and fell on top of me. He tried to wrestle me, but he was too skinny and light. "Give it to me! It's mine! Give it to me!" he shouted.

I tucked the egg into my jeans pocket. Then I rolled on top of him and pinned his arms to the floor.

I held him down till he stopped squirming and shouting.

"Give up?" I said. "Come on, Bradley. You're pinned. Say it. Give up?"

He groaned. "OK. OK. You're *crushing* me!"

I climbed to my feet and helped him up. He groaned and rubbed his skinny arms. I don't think I hurt him too bad.

"Are you going to give me the Monster Blood or not?" he asked.

"Not," I said. I patted my jeans pocket. "I'm keeping it safe and sound."

Bradley let out a cry and dived at me again. "Give it back to me, Matt! It's mine!"

That's when Livvy poked her head into the room. "What are you *doing*?" she cried. "I heard you all the way down the hall."

Bradley let go of my jeans and backed away. "None of your business, Geek Nose," he snarled.

"Huh?" Livvy's face turned an angry red.

"OK, no biggie. I'm outta here," Bradley said, fists at his sides. "You keep the Monster Blood, Matt. Go ahead. You just don't *want* me to be as big and popular as you are."

"Bradley, you don't get it," I said. "You can't eat something if you don't know what it is."

"No biggie," Bradley said again. "You keep it. But I'm keeping the birdhouse project – and I'm gonna *win* with it!"

He shoved Livvy out of his way and stomped out of the room, muttering furiously to himself.

"Whoa. What was *that* about?" Livvy said.

I pulled the egg out of my pocket and held it up to her. "It's some stupid gunk Bradley ordered online. He wanted to eat some of it, but I wouldn't let him."

"Let me see," Livvy said. She grabbed the egg and pulled it open. "Oh, sick," she moaned.

I watched it bubble over the side of the egg. "It's really gross," I said.

Livvy pushed it to my nose. "Smell it. It's totally pukey."

"Yuck." It smelled like mouldy Brussels sprouts. I hate Brussels sprouts. I grabbed the egg from Livvy's hand.

"Bradley really wanted to eat this stuff?" Livvy said.

I nodded. "He's one sick dude."

Livvy stared into the egg. "Yeah. Sick." We both heard Mom calling from downstairs. Livvy turned and ran to the stairs.

I watched the Monster Blood bubble and pop. Did people really eat this stuff? Or was this one of Bradley's crazy ideas?

I carried the egg to the window and peered down to the street. I thought maybe the two men in black might be hanging around outside. I could run out and hand them the Monster Blood.

But no. Two rabbits stood on the front lawn, up on their hind legs, frozen in headlights as a van rumbled past. No sign of the men in black.

"Whoa!" I felt the Monster Blood drip on to my hand.

I looked down. The green goo had bubbled up over the side of the egg. It poured on to my palm and began spreading to my fingers.

I dropped the egg on to my dresser. But a big blob of Monster Blood clung to my hand. It oozed over my fingers, hot and sticky. I struggled to pull it off, but it clung tightly. The putrid smell was making me ill!

What if I can't prise it off? I thought. *What if it just keeps growing on me?*

Finally, I prised the sticky stuff up and rolled it into a bubbling ball. I turned to my dresser to stuff it back into the egg.

"Whoa!" I let out a cry when I saw the green gunk pouring over the side of the dresser – into one of my ivy plants.

I glanced frantically around the room. I had to find something to hold this disgusting stuff!

My eyes stopped at something on my bottom bookshelf. Something that might be big enough and strong enough to hold the Monster Blood until I could get rid of it.

I rushed across the room. I bent down and picked up the giant china piggy bank. It was a present from my aunt Harriet. I think she won it at a carnival.

The piggy bank was bright pink. It had a coin slot on its back and a wide cork on its belly for taking the coins out. The bank was bigger than a toaster. Yes. It might hold the goo for a while.

I knew I had to be careful. I found a pair of leather gloves in my closet and slipped them on. Then I picked up the metal trowel I use for loosening the earth in my ivy pots.

I took a silver funnel I'd been using for a science experiment. I removed the cork and jammed the funnel into the hole.

I stepped up to the dresser and began shovelling up the Monster Blood. Bubbling and steaming, it clung to the trowel. I tilted it into the funnel. Now it stuck to the funnel walls.

My eyes darted around the room, searching for something that might work better. Nothing here. The stuff was too sticky.

My heart pounded as I pushed and shoved and jammed the Monster Blood into the funnel. Down through the hole in the bank's belly.

Finally, I jammed the last globs into the piggy bank. My hand trembled as I shoved in the cork. The big bank was nearly full. Would it hold the bubbling green goo?

I tossed the funnel into my closet. Then I grabbed the roll of masking tape I'd been using to build my birdhouse model. I wrapped the tape all around the bank. Strip after strip. I wrapped many strips of tape over the slot on the top.

By the time I was finished, sweat poured down my forehead. My shirt was drenched. My arms and legs were trembling.

I thought about the swim team tomorrow. The guys were all counting on me. The whole school was counting on me.

I had to calm myself down. And then I had to get to sleep. Coach Widdoes always insisted on eight hours' sleep before a meet.

I picked up the piggy bank. Heavier now. And warm. Carefully, I carried it to my closet. I tucked it into a low shelf way in the back.

Gotta calm down... Gotta stop thinking about Monster Blood...

I picked up my watering can and began drizzling water on the two ivy plants. Then I untangled some vines and misted the leaves.

Working with my plants always calms me down.

But *no way* could I stop thinking about the bubbling green gunk in the piggy bank in my closet. *I'll take it to the town dump tomorrow first thing after the swim meet*, I decided.

The dump was only two streets away. I could bury it there. No problem.

It took me a long time to fall asleep that night. I had a bunch of disturbing dreams.

I dreamed I heard strange bubbling sounds nearby.

GLUG GLUG POP GLUG GLUG.

I woke up slowly, feeling groggy, my head heavy as a rock.

GLUG GLUG POP GLUG GLUG.

The sounds from my dream! I was awake now. But I could still hear them!

Wet, smacking noises. Gurgles and pops.

It took me a long while to realize the sounds were REAL. Not a dream.

I jerked straight up in bed. My heart skipped a beat.

GLUUUG GLUG GLUUUG.

From the closet. I let out a long, worried sigh and climbed out of bed. The sick sounds grew louder as I crept across the room.

Had the Monster Blood escaped? Would it come sweeping over me in a tidal wave of hot goo?

I was two metres from the closet when I heard a scratching sound behind me. I spun around . . .

. . . *And opened my mouth in a scream of horror.*

A man! A GIANT! Eight feet tall!

He stood in my room – in front of the window, waving his outstretched arms at me!

14

"Who ARE you? What do you want?" I cried.

And then I gasped.

Moonlight flooded the window, and I saw that I wasn't staring at a giant man.

I was staring at one of my ivy plants. The one closest to the dresser. It had grown to the ceiling. Its giant tendrils were waving in the breeze from the open window.

I clicked on the ceiling light. The plant was *huge.* It creaked and groaned, bending . . . stretching. Some of the vines brushed against the ceiling!

The Monster Blood . . . I remembered it . . . dripping off the dresser into my ivy plant.

Bradley was right about one thing. The green goo really made things GROW!

This isn't fair, I thought. *It just isn't fair.*

I had practised and worked so hard for the championship meet tomorrow. And now I was getting no sleep. And I felt totally stressed and frightened.

How big would the ivy plant grow?

GLUG GLUG GLUG GLUG.

I had no choice. I had to check out the closet. I had to make sure the Monster Blood was still safe inside the piggy bank.

I stepped up to the closet. I took a deep breath – turned the knob – and pulled open the door.

"NOOOOO!" I screamed as a tall, hot wave of goo washed on to me. It bounced off my chest, then oozed into my hands.

"Oh, nooo," I groaned. *This isn't happening.* The Monster Blood spread over my hands and tightened itself like a pair of gloves.

I staggered back. My hands started to itch like crazy. The green goo tightened itself . . . tighter . . . tighter . . . I shook my hands frantically, but the hot gunk clung to my skin.

As I struggled, the Monster Blood bulged bigger. And oozed on to my chest. I swiped at it with both hands. But they were slippery, covered in green goo. I couldn't grab hold.

The hot, syrupy Monster Blood wrapped itself around my chest. Tighter . . . like a warm, tight jumper.

Gasping for breath, I squirmed and struggled.

I dropped to the rug and tried to roll it off. But it clung tight to me. And climbed higher over my body, spreading so fast. Now I could feel the sticky, warm ooze spreading on to my neck.

Tightening around my throat. Like fingers trying to strangle me.

My breath came out in loud wheezes.

I tugged at it. Twisted and bent my body. Tried to prise my fingers through the thick green blanket of goo.

Hard to breathe. . . It's . . . it's choking me!

The sickening smell poured into my nose. The gunk tickled my chin . . . rising fast.

Was it heading for my mouth?

I shut my mouth tight and gritted my teeth.

Can't breathe. . . It's BURNING me. . . CHOKING me. . .

The green goo bubbled and popped as it spread over me. The putrid aroma swept over my face. I struggled not to gag.

Desperate, I clawed at the goo over my chest. I tried desperately to dig my fingers into it . . . to pull . . . pull. . .

YES!

I plunged my fingers through the thick, wet goo. Grabbed hold. And gave it a hard tug.

YES!

It made a loud popping sound as I stretched it off my chest. I balled the sticky goo between my hands – and tugged harder.

The Monster Blood stretched like elastic, then snapped off my body into my hands. I kept rolling it into a tight ball. Tugging it off and rolling it.

I clamped the gunk between my hands, pressing it tighter, until it was the size of a basketball.

Now what?

I was still gasping for air, my heart jack-hammering.

The Monster Blood was off my body, but I could still feel its sticky warmth. Could still smell it on my itching skin.

It bubbled and popped between my hands. I staggered into the closet. Found a small duffel bag on the floor. Jammed it into the bag. Zipped the bag shut. Slammed the closet door and collapsed into my bed.

I stumbled down to breakfast the next morning. My eyes were red and burning. My head felt heavy as a rock. My whole body ached.

I stepped into the kitchen – and groaned.

Who had the nerve to show up this morning?

Three guesses, and they're all Bradley "Worm" Wormser.

He grinned at me. Like everything was just perfect between us.

"Whassup?" he said. He raised a hand to slap me a high five. But I walked right past him.

"Look, dude," Bradley said. "You don't have to share your cereal with me this morning. Your mom gave me my own bowl." He held up his cereal bowl like it was a prize.

"Thrills and chills," I muttered. I dropped into my chair across the table from him and ate my cereal. Livvy sat next to Bradley. She was mashing up her scrambled eggs with a fork. She likes to mash them flat. Don't ask me why.

I checked to make sure my mom wasn't in the kitchen. I didn't want to tell her about the Monster Blood upstairs. Dad was out of town, so he couldn't help. And I knew Mom would totally panic.

I leaned over the table. "Bradley, listen to me," I whispered. "We have a real problem."

He tilted the cereal bowl to his mouth and made loud slurping noises. Then he laughed. He thought it was a riot.

"I'm serious," I said in a loud whisper. "The Monster Blood – it's totally out of control. It made my ivy plant grow. And it—"

Bradley snapped his fingers right in front of Livvy's nose.

"Stop it!" Livvy screamed. She jabbed Bradley with her elbow. "Stop snapping in my face, Worm! I mean it!" She elbowed him again. "You hit my nose."

He laughed. "*What* nose?" he cried. "You call that pimple a nose?"

"Shut up!" Livvy shouted. "At least I don't look like a slimy worm!"

Bradley snapped his fingers in her face again.

"Bradley, listen to me." The two of them were

going at each other. I had to shout at the top of my voice. "We have to DO something! My ivy plant. . ."

Mom burst into the kitchen. "What's the racket?" she cried, covering her ears. "Go on. All of you. Get out of here. You're all going to be late."

She put a hand on my shoulder. "Dad is so sorry to miss your swim meet this afternoon. I'll try my best to be there," she said, patting me. "I'm so proud of you, Matt."

"Thanks," I muttered.

You won't be proud if I fall asleep in the pool, I thought.

For a moment, I felt like telling her everything. Telling her about my birdhouse project. About how Bradley almost got me kicked out of school. About how I had to fight the Monster Blood. How it was still upstairs in my closet, throbbing and bubbling.

Would she believe any of it?

Bradley and Livvy had already headed out the front door. There wasn't time to tell it all to her. Besides, what could Mom say? How could she help me now?

I had to find a way to deal with it.

I stuck my head out the front door. "I'll be right there!" I shouted to Livvy and Bradley.

I hurried up the stairs to my room. I wanted to check the Monster Blood one more time. I wanted to make sure it hadn't burst out of the duffel bag.

My heart was thudding in my chest as I pulled open the closet door. The ceiling light flashed on – and I let out a startled cry.

The Monster Blood! It was GONE!

I dropped to my knees and stared at the bottom shelf. Stared at the empty space where I had placed the duffel bag.

I shut my eyes. How could this happen? How could it disappear?

Finally, I climbed to my feet. I didn't want to be late on the day of the swim meet. I shut the closet door behind me.

The giant ivy plant cast a long, quivering shadow over my bed. The leaves were as big as my hand. The vines were as thick as my arms!

Deal with it later! I told myself. *Just get yourself to school. Concentrate on the swim meet. Shut this out of your mind.*

I forced my legs to move. I found Livvy waiting for me at the kerb. Bradley was already jogging across the street on his way to school.

Livvy flashed me a devilish grin. She grabbed my arm and pulled me close to whisper in my ear. "Matt, know what I did?"

"Huh?" I stared at her. "What are you talking about?"

She pulled me to the corner. Her grin hadn't faded. "I snuck into your room last night," she said. "I took that duffel bag out of the closet."

My mouth dropped open. "How did you know about it? You were *spying* on me?"

She slapped my arm. "Listen. Let me tell you what I did. This morning, I took a gob of that gooey stuff out of the bag. And guess what? I put it in Bradley's cereal!"

She tossed her head back and burst out laughing.

I almost choked. My breath caught in my throat. "How *could* you?" I cried.

She shrugged. "He deserves it," she said.

"But, Livvy, you don't understand. That stuff—"

"I know. It tastes like *yuck*," Livvy said. She giggled. "But Bradley didn't even notice. Did you *see* him? He gobbled down the whole bowl!"

She went skipping across the street to her school. I watched her meet up with three or four other girls. They were all talking at once. I wondered if Livvy would tell them about the "really awesome" joke she pulled.

Some joke. My head was spinning. Without knowing it, Bradley ate a gob of Monster Blood.

Had Livvy *poisoned* Bradley? Was he going to get horribly ill? Or WORSE?

I pictured the ivy plant spreading its enormous vines and leaves over my room. Was Bradley already ballooning up into a giant?

I gulped a deep breath of the warm morning air. Then I took off, racing to school.

Kenny and Jake – my buddies on the swim team – called to me from the corner. I gave them a quick wave, lowered my head, and kept running.

A few minutes later, I dodged through groups of kids in the halls – and burst into Mr Scotto's room.

"Bradley? Bradley?" My eyes darted frantically around the classroom. I spotted Bradley in his seat, leaning over to open his backpack. He raised his head when he heard me shouting his name.

Struggling to catch my breath, I stared at him. He looked the same. He hadn't started to grow.

I grabbed Bradley by the shoulders and began to pull him from his chair. "Hurry," I choked out. "You've got to see the nurse."

He laughed. "Have you gone wacko? I'm not ill!"

I held on to his shirt. "It's no joke," I said. "I swear. You have to go see the nurse – right now!"

He pushed my hands away. "No way," he said. "You're crazy."

Kids were staring at us. "Are they fighting again?" I heard a girl ask.

I glanced to the front of the room. Mr Scotto wasn't there yet.

I turned back to Bradley. "Please—" I said. "I'm your friend, right? Get up. Please. I'll take you to the nurse."

Bradley didn't budge. He grinned at me. "Hey, guess what?" he said.

I stared at him. "What?"

"I saw your sister put something in my cereal bowl at breakfast," Bradley said. "So, know what I did? I switched bowls with you, Matt. Ha-ha. You ate *my* cereal!"

17

Have you ever been on one of those amusement park rides that whirls around and around, and then the floor drops out from beneath you and you're left spinning in mid-air?

That's how I felt.

The whole room spun. The floor tilted up, then down.

Bradley sniggered. "Matt, you OK?"

I didn't answer. I felt weak. Dizzy.

I reeled away from him and dropped into my seat. I gazed down at my hands and feet. Was I growing?

No. Everything was still the same.

I pictured my ivy plant. Was my head going to stretch up to the ceiling in a few minutes? Was that green gook going to turn me into a total *freak* in front of the whole class?

Mr Scotto stepped into the room. He moved to the chalkboard and began talking. He pointed to a map he had drawn in yellow chalk.

What was he talking about? I don't know. I couldn't concentrate on anything he said.

I kept hearing the bubble and pop of the Monster Blood as it oozed over my dresser last night. I grabbed my stomach. Was that sick bubbling sound going to start coming from inside *me*?

I burped.

Did that mean it was starting?

The back of my neck itched.

Was it because of the Monster Blood oozing through my system?

Total panic. That's the only way I can describe how I felt. All morning, I gripped the desktop in front of me with sweaty hands. I kept checking myself out. Looking for the tiniest change. The tiniest sign. . .

I tried to force myself to listen to Mr Scotto. But now my ears started to ring. And I kept listening for the Monster Blood in my stomach to begin to bubble.

I should have been thinking about the swim meet after school.

Concentrate. That's what Coach Widdoes told me. But how could I concentrate when I kept picturing the two men in black. And remembered their warning about how dangerous Monster Blood was.

Really dangerous. And I ate a big blob of it. Thanks to my adorable sister.

The morning dragged by. I skipped lunch. Trust me, I didn't feel at all hungry.

Instead, I went to the locker room and checked out my goggles and swim gear for the meet. Actually, I went to the locker room to hide. I knew it would be empty. I didn't feel like talking to anyone.

I walked out to the swimming pool. The hot, steamy air felt good on my face. And I love the heavy chlorine smell. I bent down and touched the water. Nice temperature.

Concentrate . . . concentrate.

Mainly, I concentrated on not growing bigger. Walking back to Mr Scotto's class, I gritted my teeth and kept my stomach muscles tight. And kept checking myself out every two seconds.

The longest day of my life.

I kept glancing at the clock. Was I going to make it to the swim meet?

A little before three o'clock, my stomach started to bubble and churn. My hands started to itch. I felt hot sweat run down my forehead.

It's happening, I thought. I froze in panic. And felt a cool breeze on my legs. I looked down. Oh, noooo. . .

My bare legs stuck out of my jeans.

Did Mom shrink my jeans? I asked myself. But I knew better. I knew what was happening.

My shirt felt tight. The sleeves pinched my arms. The collar tightened around my neck.

My stomach churned. It felt like ocean waves inside me.

It's happening. It's starting to work.

My arms and legs ached. I could *feel* them growing!

The bell rang. I tried to jump up. But I was stuck in my desk! I squeezed myself free and grabbed my backpack from under my chair. The chairs suddenly looked a lot smaller.

My trainers pinched my feet. It was hard to move. But I forced myself to run. I heard Bradley call me. I didn't turn around.

I ran through the hall, my big feet pounding the floor. I wanted to get to the locker room and change before anyone saw me. Before anyone saw that I was growing taller by the minute.

My heart hammering in my chest, I burst into the locker room and ran up to the wall mirror. Oh, wow. I was at least a foot taller. How fast was I growing?

I flexed my muscles. I looked *good*! But, of course, I couldn't enjoy it. No *way* I wanted to become a giant freak in front of everyone.

Maybe, I told myself, *if I can get into the pool fast enough, I can hide my big body under the water. And no one will notice.*

I pulled on my swimming trunks. So tight. I could barely get my legs through them. I tossed a towel over my shoulders. I ducked down low. Walked stooping over.

Get to the pool, Matt. Get to the pool before anyone sees.

Almost to the pool door.

"Oh." I let out a gasp as Coach Widdoes stepped in front of me. "Hey, Matt – stop right there," he said. "You can't go in the pool!"

18

I froze. I stared at the coach. I heard my shoulders pop. They were growing. Did he hear it, too?

A smile spread over Coach Widdoes's face. "You can't go in the pool without me wishing you good luck!" he said. He slapped me a high five. "We're all counting on you, fella."

I breathed a sigh of relief. I started past him.

But he put out a hand to stop me. "Hey, have you *grown*?" he asked.

I had to think fast. "Uh . . . yeah," I said. "I've been trying to bulk up. Guess it's working."

I hurried out to the pool. The hot, steamy air greeted me along with loud voices and shouts. The team from Upper Fairmont was already taking practice laps in the water. Their coach was blowing his whistle, shouting encouragement to his swimmers.

I saw about twenty or thirty people in the bleachers at the far end. A few students. Mostly parents. I didn't spot my mom. *Maybe she got held up*, I thought.

I waved to a few of my teammates coming out of the locker room. Then I dived into the water. So far, no one had noticed how much I had changed.

I swam underwater for a lap, getting my body used to the temperature. Then I did the butterfly stroke, loosening up my arm muscles.

Halfway across the pool, I stopped. I started to tread water. I suddenly felt very strange.

I gazed at my hands. They were *huge* and growing bigger. Almost the size of a baseball glove!

I could feel my arms and legs stretching – like someone was tugging them out. My swimming trunks felt stretched to the limit, about to pop off!

I was growing FAST now – so fast I could *see* it happening.

I lowered my feet to the pool bottom. I was standing at the six-foot level. And my head was still above water!

Oh, no!

I realized why this was happening. It came to me in a flash. My ivy plant. Monster Blood had dripped on to it. And then I *watered* it.

The plant grew huge after I'd watered it.

And now here I was in the water. And as soon as I hit the water, I started to grow really fast!

I raised my eyes to the bleachers. No sign of Mom.

Good! I thought. *No way I want her to see me like this.*

The teams were lining up for the first event, the 500-metre freestyle. *My* first event. I saw the official in his black-and-white-striped shirt fiddling with his starting gun.

Can I still swim?

That was my frightening thought. *Am I too big to swim? Can I still do my normal strokes?*

I lowered my head and began to practise my breaststroke. WOW! I couldn't believe it! My speed was *amazing.* I felt so strong. I shot through the water like an attacking shark!

No human can swim this fast! I told myself. The pool suddenly appeared so tiny. I realized I could swim the length of the pool in four or five strokes!

No *way* I could lose. I was about to break every middle school swim record in history!

As long as no one sees this...

As long no one sees that I'm suddenly eight feet tall!

No time to worry about that. I floated into place between my teammates, Jake and Kenny. I bent my knees and hunched real low.

We flashed each other thumbs-up. Then we lowered our heads and got into position.

The starting gun roared, echoing off the tile walls.

The race began.

I kicked off from the pool wall and began to pull myself through the water. I reached the other wall in a few seconds and made my turn. The other swimmers were still only halfway across the pool.

I decided to take it easy on them. I swam in slow motion for a lap. But my arms were so powerful and my kicks had so much thrust, I burst forward like a rocket!

"This is AMAZING!" I couldn't hold it in. I shouted the words out loud.

I never felt so fast – so POWERFUL – in my whole life! It was *awesome*! I was a rocket! A swimming MACHINE! The fastest swimmer in the *world*!

With three laps to go, I went into full speed. I sent up a tidal wave of water as I passed the other swimmers. How far behind were they? Two whole laps!

I could hear cheers and shrieks and cries of

surprise from the bleachers. I glanced up and saw Coach Widdoes at the edge of the pool. He was bent with his hands on his knees, staring at me wide-eyed, his jaw hanging to the floor!

I made my turn and went into the final lap. *World record, here I come!*

"Ow! Hey!" I could feel myself slow down. My arm muscles began to ache.

My hands slapped the water, making loud *claps*. My big feet splashed up tall waves behind me. My arms . . . my shoulders . . . ached with pain.

I struggled to move forward. But I was bobbing on top of the water like a fat walrus!

What's happening? I wondered. *What's wrong?*

"Go! Go! Go!" I urged myself on.

Water washed through my hands as they clumsily slapped the water. My arms throbbed with pain. My kicks were sloppy, not strong enough to get me moving.

The other swimmers glided past me. I struggled to heave myself forward. But I was too heavy . . . too heavy to pull myself any further. It took all my strength not to sink to the bottom.

I'm TOO BIG! I realized. *I'm a huge, muscle-bound* blob*!*

Swimmers passed me in a blur. Kenny raised his head and flashed me a confused glance as he swam past.

My chest ached. My legs throbbed with pain.

I knew I couldn't go any further. I didn't have the strength.

Sucking a deep breath into my aching chest, I made one last, clumsy heave . . .

. . . and hit the pool wall!

It took a few seconds to hear Coach Widdoes's shouts.

What was he saying? I won? Huh? Did I really win the race?

I kept my body low underwater and raised my head. And heard the deafening screams and cheers.

"Matt – it's unbelievable! You broke the all-time record!" Coach Widdoes shouted, staring at his stopwatch.

Kenny and Jake and my other teammates swarmed around me. They slapped me high fives, splashed and hugged me, and acted like total nuts.

Cameras flashed. The screams and cheers went on and on.

I shot my fists high above my head and let out a victory cry. Winning a swim match never felt this good!

My happiness lasted another few seconds.

Then I felt cold dread sweep down over my huge body. The cheers faded from my ears. My teammates became a noisy blur.

The judge was blowing his whistle. He was trying to clear the pool for the next event.

That was my first big problem. *How do I get out of the pool without letting everyone see that I'm eight or nine feet tall? If I climb out now,* I thought, *everyone will see that I'm a giant* freak*! A monster!*

"Come on, Matt!" Kenny yelled as he headed for the locker room.

"Let's go, buddy!" Coach Widdoes smiled.

"I'll be right there." I waved them both on. "Just need to, uh, loosen up my muscles. I've got a small . . . cramp."

The pool emptied out quickly. The racers in the next event started to lower themselves into the water.

I had to move. I had to get out. But how?

I had an idea. A desperate idea.

I turned away from the crowd, kept to the side of the pool – and started walking to the deep end. I knew the pool was only eight feet deep. No problem. I was taller than that!

I walked to the deep end and glanced all around. No one watching me. They all had their eyes on the new swimmers. I climbed out and dived behind the bleachers. I stood there dripping water and listened for startled shouts. No. No one saw me.

OK. OK. I can do this, I told myself.

I slipped out the back door and made my way along the empty hall that led to the locker room. I could see the red locker room door just ahead.

Only a few metres to go.

Zzzzzzzzzip!

My tiny swimming trunks ripped – and flew off!

I backed against the wall. Totally naked.

The red locker room door seemed a mile away.

And then . . . I heard voices – GIRLS' voices! – in the hall . . . *coming my way*!

I lurched forward. My wet feet slipped on the floor. I stumbled into the door. Jerked it open – and disappeared into the locker room.

The lights were off. Grey evening light filtered in from a high window on the far wall.

The locker room was empty. Everyone was at the pool.

I made my way through the long row of lockers. I found my locker at the end. I had to bend way down to reach the combination lock. Hard to see the dial in the dim grey light.

I was alert to every sound. Water dripped in the shower room. A tree branch tapped at the window above my head. Kids were cheering another victory at the pool.

I opened my locker and snatched out my clothes. I raised my boxers and—

Too small.

They wouldn't fit around one leg.

Trembling, still dripping water, I held up my jeans and T-shirt. They looked like doll clothes.

"How can I get home?" I asked myself out loud. The words seemed to hang in the damp locker room air. "I'm totally naked. How can I get home?"

My eyes landed on a stack of towels on a bench outside the shower room. I picked up two of them, tied them together, and wrapped them around my waist.

OK. OK. At least I'm covered.

But I still can't walk home like this.

My mind raced. I felt so heavy and slow, as if I were still in the water.

I stepped up to the mirror. I was too tall to see my head without bending down! And was I still growing?

The thought sent a shiver down my body.

And then . . . I had an idea. Sometimes my scientific brain amazes even me!

OK. This idea was desperate, maybe *crazy*. But once again, I pictured my ivy plant.

I was pretty sure it was *water* that made the Monster Blood work. When I watered the plant, it started to grow. And when I jumped into the pool, my body started to stretch like crazy.

So, what if I dried myself out?

Maybe I'd shrink. Maybe I could *dry* myself back to my normal size.

My heart started to thud with excitement and hope. This could work. It really could.

Someone once told me there were hairdryers in the girls' locker room. I fumbled with the towels around my waist. Made sure they were good and tight.

Then I poked my head out into the hall. I heard shouts and cheers from the pool. No one in the hall.

My huge bare feet slapped the floor as I darted to the girls' locker room. Carefully, I pulled the door open a crack and peeked in.

Please be empty. Please be empty.

"Anyone in here?" I called. I tried to whisper, but my big new voice boomed.

Silence. No reply.

"Yesss!" I crept into the long, dark room. My first thought: it didn't smell sweaty and rank like the boys' locker room.

The lockers were all shut. The room was neat and uncluttered, except for a blue backpack resting under one bench and a pair of red and white trainers next to a wire rubbish bin.

Wow. I never thought I'd be in *here*. I kept glancing all around. What would I say if someone caught me?

I hurried to the dressing room in the back. It had a row of sinks and a mirror that covered the wall. I saw two hairdryers hanging above the sinks.

My hand trembled as I pulled one off its hook. I checked to make sure it was plugged in. Then I clicked it on.

The hairdryer whirred to life. I felt the air grow hotter as it shot out of the nozzle.

Would this work? Was I a genius? Or had I totally lost my mind?

I turned the hot air blast on to my chest. I held it there until my skin started to burn.

I aimed it at my arms and shoulders for a while. Then bent down and gave my legs a blast of hot air. Then back to my chest.

Come on! Dry me! Dry me!

I gazed into the mirror. No. Nothing changed.

I was still a nine-foot giant holding a tiny hairdryer in my big paw.

"It HAS to work!" I screamed into the mirror.

I bent to dry my legs some more.

That's when I heard the locker room door squeak open.

"Oh, no!" I gasped – and clicked off the hairdryer. I froze there with the dryer in one hand, the other hand gripping the towels around my waist.

And heard girls' voices.

I darted away from the mirror and pressed myself against the wall.

Too late.

A girl called, "Hey! What are you doing in there?"

21

I pressed myself against the cold tile wall. I held my breath.

"What are you doing?" the girl repeated.

"I'm just getting my backpack," another girl answered. "I left it in here after gym class."

"Well, hurry, Caitlin. We've already missed half the swim meet."

I didn't breathe until I heard the door close behind them. Then I let out a long whoosh of air.

A close call.

I placed the hairdryer back on its hook. My big idea was a total flop. I tightened the towels around my waist.

I had to get help. I had to get home and think.

I crept through the school quickly and hurried out the back door. The sun had fallen behind the trees. The air was cool and damp.

Maybe, I thought, *if I keep low behind hedges and bushes... Maybe I can get home without being seen.*

* * *

Yes. I made it home.

I crept up to the kitchen door and peered through the window. No sign of Mom. I pushed open the door and jumped inside.

The kitchen was warm and smelled of chocolate. I was never so happy to be here.

I checked out the living room and the den. No one there. I knew Livvy was at her friend Martha's house. Was Mom at the swim meet, waiting for me to compete in my next event?

I couldn't think about that now. I had to think about only one thing: finding an antidote to the Monster Blood. Shrinking myself back to my good old five feet two.

The house looked so small. I knew I wouldn't even *fit* at the kitchen table. I lumbered up to my room. My huge legs were still aching from my mad dash home.

I shut my eyes before I stepped into my room. *Please, please let the ivy plant be back to its normal size.*

No. It stretched along the ceiling, its big leaves shading the ceiling light.

My bed cracked as I dropped on to it. One of the legs fell off. I sighed. I was too heavy for my own bed.

Wait. Another idea.

Maybe Bradley could help me. I remembered what

he said when he first showed me the Monster Blood. The green plastic egg came inside a box.

Did Bradley save the box? Maybe it had instructions on how to get small again.

My mobile sat next to my iPod docking station on the night stand. I grabbed it up and flipped it open. I knew Bradley's mobile number by heart.

I jabbed at the keys. Jabbed. Poked.

Oh, no.

My finger was too big. It hit three or four keys at once.

I let out an angry shout and heaved the phone against the wall.

I have to go next door and see him, I decided. *But I can't go in these towels.*

I opened my closet. My eyes frantically raced over my clothes. All too small.

Then I remembered my dad's big, old raincoat. He found it at a thrift shop and wore it as a joke. He always said it was big enough for two people!

Did Mom keep it? Was it still in the closet in the basement?

The stairs creaked and cracked under my weight as I lumbered downstairs. I found the old raincoat in the basement closet. It stunk of mothballs. But I didn't care. I pulled it around me and tied the belt. The huge coat fitted perfectly!

I pulled my bulky body up the stairs. My feet were so big, they poked over the steps.

"Bradley, I hope you're home," I muttered. "And I hope you kept that Monster Blood box."

I pulled open the front door – and let out a shriek.

The two men dressed in black! They cried out, too, when they saw me. And backed off the porch, gaping at me.

"You – you're ten feet tall!" one of them gasped.

At first, I was startled to see them. Frightened. But I quickly realized they could help me. They were just the help I needed.

"Look at me!" I cried. "I'm a giant freak. I admit it. I have what you've been looking for!"

They stared at me with their mouths open. They didn't say a word.

"I have the Monster Blood!" I boomed. "Look what it did to me! Do you know how to help me?"

My big voice cracked. "Please help me!" I cried. "I promise – I'll give the Monster Blood back!"

They both narrowed their eyes at me.

"Monster Blood?" one of them said. "What on *earth* is Monster Blood?"

22

It was my turn to stare at *them* with my mouth hanging open. “Monster Blood,” I finally choked out. “You know. The stuff you want me to return?”

They exchanged glances. “We don’t know anything about that,” the man with all the rings said. “We work for the company that makes the Gas Attack cans.”

“A bad batch was sent out,” his partner said. “It’s way too smelly. It can make people really ill.”

“Did you order it?” the first man asked. “We’ll give you your money back.”

I let out a long sigh. These men were not going to help me at all. “You’ve got the wrong guy,” I said, shaking my head sadly. “My neighbour ordered the Gas Attack. We already used it. It was disgusting, but we’re OK.”

“Sorry we bothered you,” Ring Fingers said. They turned and hurried to their car. As he pulled open the door, he shouted back at me, "Good luck, kid. Ever think of playing basketball?"

Ha-ha. Very funny.

I watched them drive away. Then I tightened the raincoat belt and ran across the front garden to Bradley's house.

"OWWW!" I let out a cry as my head bumped a low tree branch. Whoa. Guess you have to duck a *lot* when you're nine feet tall!

I climbed the porch and pounded on Bradley's front door. "You've GOT to have that box," I muttered. "You've GOT to have the instructions."

Bradley pulled open the door. His eyes bulged in horror and he let out a terrified shriek. "A GIANT!" he wailed. "Get away – *now*! I'm calling the police!"

"N-no—" I stammered.

He slammed the door in my face.

"No! It's *me*!" I pounded the front door again, with both fists.

The door cracked. I saw the hinges fly off. And the door fell in with a thud.

I didn't know my own strength!

I heard a deafening siren. The burglar alarm!

Bradley stood there trembling in the front hall, eyes still bulging. He started to back away.

"Bradley, it's ME!" I shouted over the blaring alarm siren. "It's Matt. The Monster Blood did this to me. You've got to help me!"

He squinted up at me. "Matt?" he squeaked. "R-really?"

I thundered over to him. "Where is the Monster Blood box? Bradley, do you still have the box?"

"I – I might," he stammered. "Up in my room." He turned and began running up the stairs.

I tried to follow him up, but – *CRASH!* – my head bumped the ceiling. No way I could fit on the stairs.

The burglar alarm continued to blare, rising and falling. I stared up to the second floor. "Do you have it? Can you find it?"

And then I heard other sirens. From out on the street.

The police! They must be responding to the burglar alarm!

I froze in panic. "Bradley – hurry!" I screamed.

I couldn't let the police see me like this! Crazy thoughts flew through my head. What if they thought I was a giant from outer space? What if they shot first and asked questions later?

I had to get out of here.

I spun away from the stairs – and saw two police patrol cars pull to the kerb in front of the house.

"Bradley? Where *are* you?" I screamed. "Bradley?"

23

Three uniformed cops raced up the front walk.

Ducking under the ceiling light, I took off. To the back of Bradley's house.

"Police officers!" a deep voice shouted from the busted front door.

Did they see me? I heaved open the kitchen door and crept across the garden towards my house.

Halfway there, I heard footsteps. Heavy breathing. A shadow came up from behind mine on the grass.

The police! NO!

I spun around to face them.

"Hey! Bradley – it's you!" I cried.

"I – I've got the box," Bradley whispered. He held it up to me. A green box with MONSTER BLOOD in dripping red letters.

"Come on. Hurry," I said. I ran to my kitchen door.

I pulled it open and ducked my head to go inside.

"Huh?" Wait! I froze in surprise.

I didn't have to duck. I fitted into the doorway.

I grabbed the door and held on tight. Something was pulling me down. Something invisible . . . tightening . . . holding me down . . . pressing me . . . *flattening* me!

My whole body ached. I let out groan after groan.

I gasped when I realized I was shrinking.

I watched my big hands grow smaller, like balloons losing their air.

My arms pulled in. The floor seemed to rise up. But I knew I was sinking down. Folding in . . . dropping . . . dropping. . .

In seconds, I would be just a few inches taller than Bradley. Still shrinking . . . sinking into the huge raincoat . . . disappearing.

Disappearing?

Yes! I was shrinking too fast. Shrinking too far! In a few seconds, I'd be the size of a bug. And then . . . GONE!

"Help me! Help me!" I screamed. I tried to pull myself upright. Tried to stand tall. Tried to *stretch* myself up.

But I couldn't fight the wave pulling me down.

I gripped the sides of the door. I tried to fight off the panic that swept over me.

Tightened my throat. Kept me from taking a breath.

Total, mind-numbing panic.

I watched Bradley appear to grow taller . . . taller.

And I knew I couldn't stop myself.

In a few seconds, I would disappear for ever.

The floor swooped up beneath me. The kitchen light suddenly seemed far away. I felt like a tiny mouse, peering up at the ceiling.

"Do something!" I screamed at Bradley. "I can't stop shrinking!"

He gaped at me, eyes rolling wildly in his head.

"Read the Monster Blood box!" I shouted. "What does it say? Read it!"

Bradley's hands were shaking as he pulled the box to his face. He twirled it between his hands, searching for instructions. He dropped it. The box hit the floor. He bent to pick it up – and stepped on it.

"Hurry!" I pleaded. I could feel my bones pulling in . . . my skin tightening. . . "Whoa, wait. I found something," Bradley said finally. He began reading from the side of the box:

"'We hope you enjoy this sample twelve-hour version of MONSTER BLOOD. But for more exciting results, use this coupon for twenty per cent off on new, improved, **LONG-LASTING** MONSTER BLOOD!'"

"It's just a sample!" I cried happily. "Yes! Yes! Just a sample – and it's wearing off!"

I ran to the hallway mirror. I gaped at my reflection. Yesss! I was back to my normal height.

"Excellent!" I turned and slapped Bradley a high five. Then we bumped knuckles. "I'm back! I'm back!" I cried.

I hurried to the stairs. "Let's check out my ivy plant," I said. "I'll bet it's smaller, too."

Bradley followed me upstairs. I could still hear the alarm siren wailing next door.

"Whoa!" Bradley stopped short in the doorway to my room and let out a cry. The ivy plant still climbed over the ceiling. It hadn't shrunk like me.

"It – it's like something in the *jungle*!" Bradley cried.

"I guess Monster Blood works differently on plants," I said.

I didn't care. I was back to normal.

We returned to the kitchen – and Mom came bursting in. "Oh, thank goodness! You're both safe!" she cried. "There was a robbery next door. The robbers broke down the front door. But they didn't take anything."

"I . . . I know," I said. "I went next door, Mom, and—"

"To help Bradley?" Mom cried. "You risked your life to help Bradley? Matt – that's so wonderful of you!" She wrapped me in a hug.

Should I tell her the truth? Should I tell her what *really* happened?

No way. She'd never believe it.

That night in my room, I cut back the leaves on my ivy plant so I could get to my worktable. I felt great. No. I felt *better* than great.

I was back to normal. I'd set the world record in the 500-metre freestyle. And now I wanted to win Mr Scotto's Science Prize.

I began fitting the sides of my birdhouse together. I already had the computer wiring ready to install. I knew I could build the winning project.

No way could Bradley build one as good as mine. . .

25

The next morning, Mom drove me to school with my science project.

I carried it carefully between my hands, into the gym. Dozens of kids were already there. Long tables had been set up under one basketball net.

The big room was quiet. Kids were busy setting up their projects.

I carried the birdhouse down the first aisle, looking for a place to put it down. I stopped next to Shawn Deere, a brainy girl in our class I liked a lot. She was attaching a water hose to the back of a tall plastic box.

I had to ask. "Shawn, what is it?"

She didn't look up. She concentrated on the hose. "It's a waterfall that flows UP," she said. "I'm trying to prove that gravity doesn't exist."

"Cool," I said. I moved down the table. Another kid was slipping batteries into a complicated metal contraption. It looked like an insect with a dozen legs. "It's a Self-Destruction Machine," he told me. "When I turn it on, it totally destroys itself."

"Awesome," I said.

I still thought my birdhouse had a good chance of winning. It was simple and useful, and it really worked. I set it up at the end of the table and checked out the computer functions. When I showed it off to Mr Scotto, I wanted everything to work without a glitch.

A short while later, Mr Scotto came down the aisle. He studied each project and made notes on a long clipboard.

Since I was at the end of the table, he saw my birdhouse last. He was definitely impressed by the temperature control and the built-in rain guard. He grinned when I showed off the computerized seed feeder.

"Matt, you've taken Bradley's idea to a new level," he said. "Great imagination. And the computer programming is *brilliant*!"

"Thank you," I said. I could feel my heart start to race. I was excited.

"I have to give a few projects a second look," he whispered. "And I'll need to see Bradley's birdhouse. But I think yours is the winner."

He moved back up the aisle. I wanted to cheer and jump up and down in triumph. But I knew I had to wait for that.

I gazed down the rows of tables. Whoa. Wait. Where was Bradley?

"I don't believe it," I muttered. Bradley hadn't even shown up!

I guessed he couldn't get his birdhouse to work. Or maybe he realized he couldn't win with a stolen idea.

I saw Mr Scotto striding back down the row towards me. He had a big smile on his face. And he carried a silver trophy in his hands. I knew he was about to make the big announcement.

"Matt—" he said.

And then the gym doors burst open. And I saw a giant tree crash through the doorway.

No. Not a tree.

It took me a few seconds to recognize my huge ivy plant. Its tendrils stretched out like tree branches. The huge leaves bobbed and shook like a ship's sails!

Bradley dropped the pot to the floor. He stepped out from behind the monster plant. "Ta-DAA!" he sang. "Mr Scotto, I made this plant grow big by using ultraviolet laser light beams!"

What a liar.

Oohs and aahs rose up and echoed off the high gym walls. Some kids started to clap. Kids were gaping at the giant plant and crying out in disbelief.

The ivy plant bobbed in its pot like some kind of movie monster. Glowing under the lights, the fat leaves shimmered and shook.

The tendrils curled and uncurled like long green snakes.

Mr Scotto handed Bradley the silver trophy. "Our WINNER!"

Cheers rang out.

I didn't cheer. I was too stunned to do anything. I had to grab the tabletop to keep from falling to the floor.

I can't let Bradley get away with this, I decided. *I can't let him win with this lie. He's a total cheater. And, it isn't even his ivy plant – it's MINE!*

I started over to Bradley and Mr Scotto. I had to tell Mr Scotto the truth about Bradley's project. I had to stop this.

But halfway across the gym, I looked down. And saw one of the long snakelike tendrils curl around Bradley's ankle.

Bradley was waving the trophy over his head, enjoying the cheers and applause. He didn't seem to notice.

Another long tendril stretched . . . stretched . . . and wrapped itself around Bradley's knee.

Bradley held the trophy in front of him and posed for pictures. Cameras flashed. Bradley's grin grew wider.

I watched a thick tendril wrap itself around Bradley's waist. Another one curled around his thigh. Bradley was in major trouble and had no idea! Would he ever escape?

I decided I'd better hurry.

I pushed past the crowd of newspaper photographers and shook Bradley's hand. "Congratulations!" I said. "You deserve it, Bradley. You really do!"

ENTER HORRORLAND

ADMIT ONE
WHERE NIGHTMARES COME TO LIFE!
HorrorLand

THE STORY SO FAR . . .

After his battle with Monster Blood, Matt was thrilled to receive a surprise invitation to HorrorLand theme park. One of the Horrors even gave him a special key card that helped him win every game. Matt's luck was improving fast. Or so he thought.

Matt soon met Billy and Sheena Deep. They found a café where they saw their missing friends, Britney and Molly, behind a large window. Matt used his key card to enter the mysterious café – and gasped! Britney and Molly were gone. . .

And Sheena became invisible!

What's next? Turn the page to join Matt in HorrorLand. . .

1

Kids who know me – Matt Daniels – know that I can handle things. I mean, if you grow to nine feet tall in under an hour, you can pretty much handle anything.

But here I was, staring into the mirror in this tiny café in the HorrorLand hotel. Two girls had vanished into thin air. Another girl stood right beside us – and we couldn't see her!

No way I could get my head around *this*!

I froze. I kept blinking. But I couldn't make the room stop spinning.

They do a lot of weird stuff at HorrorLand. It's a scary theme park, I told myself. *It's supposed to be creepy.*

But is turning kids invisible one of their tricks? My heart pounded. *Or is something really dangerous going on?*

In front of me, the big mirror on the café wall shimmered and bubbled – as if it were *alive*!

I swung away from the mirror and stared at this kid I'd just met. Billy Deep. He and his sister had received a surprise invitation to HorrorLand, too. Now he didn't look happy about it. Billy's mouth hung open, and his eyes were popping out of his head. He looked scared.

The café stood empty. Just rows of little tables with blue-and-white-chequered tablecloths.

"Help me!" Sheena screamed. "Matt! Billy! You've got to *do* something! I'm invisible!"

"I – I don't understand—" Billy stammered. He was having a lot of trouble getting the words out.

I could feel my heart thudding in my chest. I struggled to think clearly.

I'm a science freak. I knew there had to be a scientific answer for what was going on here. "Is it some kind of trick mirror?" I asked.

"When we came into the café, I . . . I touched the mirror," Sheena said in a shaky voice. "I thought I saw Britney and Molly in it. The mirror felt weird. Kinda soft and . . . and warm."

"So it *is* a trick mirror!" I cried. I rushed forward and stuck out my hand.

"HEY!" I shouted as my hand sank into the mirror.

The mirror *was* soft and warm. Kind of sticky. My hand plunged in wrist deep. And I could feel the thick liquid pulling my arm deeper.

"No way!" I shouted, and jerked my hand away.

Billy ran up beside me and pressed his hand to the mirror. He pounded it with his fist. We both pounded.

Solid glass now.

"This *has* to be a trick," I said. "But how can it be soft like liquid one second and then—"

"Forget about the mirror!" Sheena screamed. "Do something to help me! Did you forget? I'm *invisible*! You've got to help me!"

I didn't blame her for losing it. But I suddenly had another thought.

"Maybe Britney and Molly are standing here," I said. "Like Sheena. Only they're invisible, too."

"Huh?" Billy squinted at me.

I started to shout.

Then he joined in. "Molly? Britney? Are you here?"

"Can you hear us? Britney? Molly?" I said. "Are you still in the café with us? Are you here?"

Silence.

It was so quiet, I could hear the blood pulsing in my ears.

I felt Sheena tug my arm. “Hurry,” she said. “We have to find help.”

Billy and I darted to the café door. I knew Sheena was right behind us. I could hear her footsteps on the tile floor.

We burst out into the long hotel hall. Spiderwebs hung from the ceiling. The black and white wallpaper was covered with grinning skulls.

But who cared about that fake stuff? We had a *real* problem to deal with.

“The Horror at the front desk will know what to do,” Billy said. He swallowed and then added in a tiny voice, “I hope.”

“He refused to help us before,” Sheena said.

“This is different,” I said. “This time—”

We turned a corner and bumped into two Horrors. They wore orange and black uniforms and had silver badges on their caps. MPs – Monster Police.

I read their name tags. The tall redheaded one was named Benson. His chubby partner was named Clem. Clem had purple horns that curled out from his forehead.

I had run into MPs before. A bunch of different MPs had chased me through the park. They were trying to take away the strange plastic room key card another Horror had given me. I had it tucked safely in my jeans pocket.

They were scary dudes. But this time, I was glad to see these guys. "We need your help," I said, breathing hard.

"Front desk is that way," the Horror Cop named Benson said, pointing down the hall.

"You don't understand," I said. "We have a problem. Billy's sister is invisible."

The two MPs squinted at us. Clem reached up and scratched his left horn. Benson laughed. "You're joking, right?"

Clem grinned at his partner. "What did the doctor say to the Invisible Man? Sorry, I can't see you now."

They both laughed.

"It isn't a JOKE!" Sheena screamed.

They didn't seem to hear her.

"It isn't a joke," Billy repeated. "We went into that restaurant down the hall, and my sister went invisible. I'm *serious*."

Their smiles faded. Beneath his horns, Clem had bright yellow eyes. He stared hard at Billy. "Where is your sister?"

"I'm standing right here!"

I heard Sheena, but the two Horror MPs didn't. Were they *pretending* they didn't hear her? Or was this some kind of HorrorLand magic where only Billy and I could hear Sheena?

"She's standing right in front of you," I told them. "Two other girls completely disappeared when we went into the café. We're not making this up."

"Is this just a HorrorLand trick?" Billy asked. "You know. Something you do to scare us?"

The two Horrors didn't answer his question.

"You said two girls disappeared?" Clem asked, narrowing his yellow eyes at Billy and me.

"We saw them in the mirror," I said. "But then—"

"Mirror? *What* mirror?" Benson boomed.

The two MPs tensed. They stepped closer. I could see something had upset them.

Benson planted his hands at his waist. "Where did this happen?" he asked.

"I *told* you. In the little café. Around the corner," Billy said.

"Are you going to help me or not?" Sheena cried.

Clem scratched his horn again. "Café?"

"Take us there," Benson ordered. "Show us this café with the mirror."

"And then you'll help my sister?" Billy asked.

"Sure, sure," Clem muttered.

Benson pushed the cap back on his head. "Just take us there," he said.

I led the way. It wasn't a long walk, but it seemed like miles. I felt really bad for Sheena. I could hear her breathing hard. I knew how frightened she must feel.

We ducked under a thick knot of fake spiderwebs. Down the hall, I heard evil laughter, then kids shrieking and laughing.

HorrorLand is supposed *to be about fun and laughing*, I thought. *Kids aren't supposed to disappear and go invisible.*

Something had gone terribly wrong.

I wondered if these two Horror Cops had any idea how to help us.

We turned the corner and walked halfway down the hall. The two MPs followed close behind us, eyes straight ahead.

"Here," Billy said, stopping. "The little café – it was right here. I remember. . ."

My mouth suddenly felt dry. Again, I could hear the blood pulsing in my ears.

The café had vanished.

Nothing there but solid wall.

"It HAS to be here!" Sheena wailed. "It HAS to!"

Billy turned to me. "Did we go down the wrong hall?"

I shook my head. "It was here. Right here." I pounded the wallpaper with my fist. Nothing but solid wall behind it.

Billy jogged down the hall, running his hand against the wall. I guess he was feeling for a door or something.

After a few seconds, he returned, his eyes wide with fright.

Clem scowled at Billy and me. "There's never been a café here," he said. "What kind of game are you kids playing?"

"It's NOT a game!" Sheena screamed. "The café was right here! Can't you hear me?"

I decided to try to reason with them. "Dudes, we're not making this up," I said. "There really was a café here. Two girls really did disappear. And Billy's sister—"

"She's standing right here," Billy told them.

"Are you going to help us or not?" I demanded.

The two MPs moved to the wall. They started whispering to each other. All the while, they kept their eyes on us.

Finally, Benson waved us forward. "Follow me, kids," he said. "Sorry it took us so long. I think Sergeant Clem and I can help you. Come with us to the lab."

"Thank goodness!" Billy cried. He pumped his fist in the air. "Do you really think you can bring my sister back?"

"Probably," Benson muttered. He and his partner began walking fast. Billy and I had to run to keep up with them. We turned a corner and hurried down another long, dark hall.

I heard Sheena running between Billy and me. "Are you sure we can trust them?" she asked.

"Do we have a choice?" Billy replied.

Benson led us to the end of the hall. He stopped in front of wide double doors. A sign on the wall read: DETECTION CHAMBER.

Clem slid a green key card into a slot and the doors started to slide open. "In here," he ordered, waving us through.

I held back. "Why are we going in here?" I asked.

"We need to detect the invisible girl," Clem said.

"If we can't see or hear her, we can't make her visible again."

It seemed to make sense. We followed them through the doorway.

I let out a gasp as my eyes adjusted to the dim light. The huge room didn't look like a lab. It looked like a horror-movie torture chamber!

The first thing I saw was a tall chair with red and blue wires poking out of it – like an *electric chair*! Beside it stood a tall wooden frame with a blade across the top. A guillotine?

A cone of light spilled over a long white table. Thick leather straps lay across the table. A cabinet beside it was loaded with shiny steel tools.

Against the wall, dark machines hummed. A stack of metal cages – the size of dog crates – stood in the centre of the room. A shrill hissing sound filled the air.

I poked Billy in the side. "Let's get out of here," I said.

I turned. The doors had already slid shut behind us.

A chill shot down my back. "What *is* this place?" I shouted. "Why did you bring us here?"

"To help you," Clem said. He pulled out a low metal table. Like a doctor's examining table. The table had red and black dials along one side.

He began messing with wires underneath it.

"We know how to help you with your problem," Benson said. He stepped up close to Billy and me. He gazed at Billy for a long time. Then he turned to me.

"We only want to help you," Benson said. Behind him, Clem pushed a plug into a socket. The dials on the metal table lit up.

"We know why you're having problems," Benson said softly. "You have something that doesn't belong to you."

Whoa. I knew *instantly* what he was talking about.

The room key card. The strange card I had hidden in my pocket.

"Hand it to us right now," Clem said. He stuck out his big hand. It was covered with red and purple warts. "Hand it to me, and your problems will be over. I swear."

Why didn't I believe him?

Because he was a terrible liar. He couldn't keep a grin off his face.

"Trust us," Benson said. "We're here to help you. We want every guest to have a great time here in HorrorLand."

Billy and I didn't move.

Clem tugged at one of his curly horns. Then he stuck out his warty hand again. "One of you has what we're looking for. Hand it over now. Don't make us *take* it from you."

No way was I going to let them take the key card!

I wasn't going to give it back until I knew why they wanted it so badly.

No way. No *way*!

But what could I do?

4

My legs were shaking but I stood very still. I stared back at the two MPs, trying to look tough.

I could see Billy trembling beside me. He knew what the two Horrors wanted. But he didn't say a word.

Clem grabbed Billy by the shoulders. He was gentle, not rough. But he pushed Billy to the metal table.

"Sorry we have to do it this way," he said. "It would be so much easier if you just hand it over."

"I . . . don't know what you mean," Billy stammered. "Really. I don't *have* anything."

"Lie down on the table," Clem said. "Now!"

"Let him GO!" Sheena screamed.

Again, the Horrors didn't hear her.

Clem had his big, warty hands under Billy's armpits. He started to lift him on to the metal table.

"What are you *doing* to me?" Billy cried.

"Relax, kid," Benson said. "We're not going to hurt you. It's an X-ray machine. That's all."

"An X-ray machine?" Billy cried. "But—"

"One of you has what we're looking for," Benson said. "The X-ray machine will find it. Just relax. This won't even take a minute."

I watched Clem lift Billy on to the X-ray table.

Wow, I thought. *If they're going to all this trouble, my key card must be something* really *special.* My brain whirred. *What could be so important about it*?

As Clem loomed over the table, Billy sprawled on his back, arms tight at his side. "Don't move a muscle," Clem ordered.

Benson twirled some dials on the side of the table. He glanced at a video screen on the wall. I could see Billy's bones on the X-ray screen. And I could see a pack of chewing gum in one of his pockets.

"He doesn't have it," Benson told his partner.

Clem gently lifted Billy off the table and set him down on the floor. "Thanks, kid," Clem said. "Sorry if I scared you."

Billy shook his head. He brushed back his dark hair. He looked at me, but he didn't say anything.

Clem waved me to the table. "You're next, pal."

My legs were shaky and my heart was thumping like crazy. But *no way* I'd let them know I was scared.

"No problem," I said.

I didn't wait for them. I climbed on to the table.

I lay flat on my back and pressed my hands against the cool metal. I couldn't see the video screen from here. But I knew the two MPs were studying it.

The room grew silent. I could hear the hum of the machines behind me and the pop and hiss of steam across the room.

"This kid doesn't have it, either," Benson said finally. "Let him up."

Clem pulled me to my feet. I couldn't keep a smile off my face as I stepped beside Billy. These dudes were pretty easy to fool.

"Can we go now?" Billy asked.

Clem raised a warty paw. "Not so fast," he said. "Let's talk about this mirror you think you saw."

I grabbed Billy's arm and tugged. "Let's go."

Our shoes clattered against the hard floor as we ran towards the double doors. I turned and saw the two MPs take off, lumbering after us.

"Hey!" Clem let out a cry as he stumbled over something and toppled to the floor. Benson fell over him and hit his head on the X-ray table as he went down.

I heard Sheena laugh. "I *tripped* him!" she cried. "*Now* maybe he believes I'm here!"

The two Horrors were scrambling to their feet. We didn't have much time.

I tried the handles on the double doors. The doors wouldn't budge.

"Sheena, quick—" I said. "Give me back the key card. Maybe it'll work."

Yes, that's how I fooled the X-ray machine. I slipped the key card to Sheena. She hid it in her fist, and it became invisible, too.

Now it appeared to float towards me. I grabbed it and shoved it into a slot beside the doors.

Great! The card worked again! The doors hummed loudly, then slid open with a *whoosh.*

We burst out of the lab and took off running down the hall. I pushed open the back door of the hotel and leaped outside. Clouds covered the sky. The air felt cool and damp.

Kids and families roamed over Zombie Plaza. "Come on!" I said, tugging Billy. "We've got to lose ourselves in the crowd."

"But – how?" Billy cried. "The two MPs – they're right behind us."

I glanced back. They were running full speed after us, shouting, "Stop those kids! Stop them!"

I forced myself to run. We thudded past a mask store. Then a store called IT'S A HOWL. As we ran past, frightening howls poured out through the open door.

No place to hide.

"Stop those kids!" the Horrors shouted, close behind us.

I turned – and almost bumped into a cart filled with shrunken heads.

"They're going to catch you," Sheena said, close beside me. "Should I try to trip them again?"

"No. Over there," I said, pointing. I had an idea.

We darted through groups of kids in the centre of the plaza. Up ahead, I saw a long line of people waiting to get into the Haunted Theatre.

"Get in line! Hurry! Get in line!" I cried.

We stepped into the back of the line. I hoped the MPs wouldn't look for two guys standing in line for the theatre.

Billy and I were both gasping for breath. The line started to move forward.

"Look normal," I said. "Don't look back. Don't look for those two Horrors."

"But – but—" Billy sputtered. He bumped my shoulder.

I turned and saw Clem and Benson moving towards us. Their heads were lowered. Their eyes were locked on us.

OK, OK. So *every* plan isn't brilliant. I never said I was perfect.

The three of us took off running again. Across from the theatre, I saw a narrow grey building with no windows. The letters on the sign above the entrance looked like dripping blood. It read: DR TWISTED'S SCIENCE LAB.

"Go," I whispered. We darted in through the narrow door.

Dark inside. Silent and empty. I blinked hard, waiting for my eyes to adjust.

We were standing in a long, narrow room with black walls. Red and green glass tubes twisted over our heads. A spotlight poured dim light down on a narrow lab table, complete with bubbling beakers and glowing test tubes.

A skeleton in a white lab coat hunched over one end of the table. He was pouring green gas from one beaker to another.

"Welcome to my lab," he said in a tinny recorded voice. "You're just in time for my latest experiment. In fact, you ARE my latest experiment! Hahahaha!"

"Whoa. We just *escaped* a lab like this," Sheena said, still breathing hard.

"Only *that* one was real," I said. "This one is all fake."

We heard voices from outside. We ducked behind the table and dropped to our knees. I took a deep breath and held it.

A few seconds later, I heard hard footsteps, then Clem's voice. "Did they come in here?"

"No. I told you. They ran into the theatre," Benson answered.

They shuffled away. I realized I was still holding my breath. I let it out slowly, then climbed to my feet.

I leaned on the lab table, trying to steady myself. "We lost them," I muttered.

"Welcome to my lab. You're just in time for my latest experiment. . ." The skeleton's speech began to roll again.

"Now what?" Billy asked softly.

"I just don't get it," Sheena said. "Why won't the Horrors help us? Why don't they believe us? We told them two girls are missing and that I'm invisible. And they didn't seem to care at all. All they cared about was taking Matt's key card away."

"Hey, check this out," Billy said. He was staring at big glass jars on a low shelf. "Are those *real* animal heads in those jars?"

"Nothing is real in here," I said. "It's all a joke."

"In fact, you ARE my latest experiment! Hahahaha!" the skeleton doctor repeated. Green gas floated from his beaker.

"We have to get out of here," I said.

Billy picked up a box from the shelf. "Weird," he whispered. "It says 'TRY ME'."

I squinted at the big words on the green box with dripping red letters that spelled out MONSTER BLOOD.

Billy started to pull up the lid.

"NOOOOO!" I screamed. "DON'T OPEN IT!"

My scream startled Billy. He dropped the box.

It hit the floor hard, and the lid popped open.

"Oh, no!" Billy and Sheena both cried out as the green goop bubbled up from the box.

Making squishy sucking sounds, the Monster Blood spread across the floor at our feet. Then it started to grow, rising up quickly. Standing up as if *alive*!

I jumped back in horror. My mind was spinning. *How could there be Monster Blood in HorrorLand?*

Billy bent down and frantically tried to shove the green gunk back into the box. But it had spread too quickly. It plopped over his shoes and started to climb his leg.

"Get it off me!" he screamed, kicking and thrashing his legs.

"Just run!" I said. I tugged him by the arm. "It's growing too fast! Let's *go*!"

"I . . . I can't. It's wrapping around my legs!" Billy cried.

Billy reached down and tried to pull it off with both hands. But his hands stuck in the thick, bubbling slime. In seconds, they disappeared into the Monster Blood.

"Help me! Get it off!" he wailed.

And then I saw the outline of two hands shoot into the bubbling Monster Blood. Sheena's hands! Trying to rescue her brother.

"It's too sticky. It won't come off!" she said. She gasped as the thick green gel rolled around her arms.

I couldn't see Sheena. But I could see her hands grappling with the goo. And I could see her struggling to pull her arms free.

I froze, staring in horror as the Monster Blood covered both of them, popping and bubbling.

"It . . . it's *swallowing* us!" Billy cried. "Matt! Help! It's swallowing us both!"

How could this happen? How could Monster Blood follow me here?

I wanted to help my friends. But I knew if I grabbed the stuff, it would stick to me and pull me in, too.

What could I do?

My hands tensed at my sides. I watched them kicking and twisting their bodies, struggling against the fast-rising goo.

The key card.

My hand slid to my jeans pocket. Yes! The strange card had helped me out before. Maybe... Maybe it could help us one more time.

My hand was shaking. I struggled to slide it out of my pocket.

I raised it high. I aimed the front of the card at Billy and Sheena and held it there.

Nothing happened.

The Monster Blood oozed up towards Billy's

neck and shoulders. His dark eyes bulged. His mouth was wide in a silent scream of terror.

I could see the outline of Sheena's hands and arms as she fought to untangle herself, twisting and squirming.

"Help us! Matt – DO something!"

I turned the card around and tried again. Nothing.

I pushed the card closer, till it almost touched the Monster Blood.

"Come on – work! WORK!" I pleaded.

But no. The card wasn't helping at all.

"Matt – it's . . . up to my *chin*!" Billy wailed.

"So sticky. . . Can't breathe. . ." Sheena's voice came out in a choked whisper.

I still had the key card raised in front of me when a loud voice boomed from the lab entrance. "WHAT'S GOING ON IN HERE?"

"Huh?" Startled, I spun around hard and almost fell. A tall giant of a Horror burst into the lab – big hairy hands balled into fists.

He had short yellow horns on his head, with wavy green hair falling over his boulder-like forehead. He had bright blue eyes under thick brown eyebrows.

I recognized him. Yes. As he tromped closer, I read the brass name tag on his purple and green uniform: BYRON.

Byron was the Horror who came up to me when I first arrived. He was the Horror who slipped me the key card.

"What *is* this? What have you done?" he shouted in his booming deep voice.

I pointed to my struggling friends. Billy and Sheena were almost buried under the throbbing green mound of Monster Blood. "Can you help them? Can you do something?" I cried.

Byron frowned. His eyes studied the pulsing green goo. Then he turned back to me.

"Sorry," he said softly. "Better say goodbye. It's too late for them."

I gasped. My breath caught in my throat.

Byron blinked. His blue eyes narrowed. He snapped his hairy fingers. "Oh, wait," he said. "I think I might have something that should help."

He reached into his uniform and pulled out a small square object. At first, I thought it was another key card. But then I saw the light bounce off it, and I knew what it was.

A mirror. A small pocket mirror.

"This should do it," Byron said to me. He turned the little mirror and aimed it at the throbbing mound of Monster Blood.

I heard a loud *pop*.

The pile of green goop stopped oozing and bubbling. And as I gaped in amazement, the Monster Blood spilled away from Billy and Sheena.

And began to pour over the mirror.

It took a few seconds for me to realize that the stuff was being *sucked* into the mirror.

But, yes! Yes! It came rolling off Billy and

Sheena, like an ocean wave sweeping away. My heart pounding, I watched it pour into the mirror in a steady green stream.

Seconds later, Billy stood in front of us, pulling a few sticky gobs of Monster Blood off his T-shirt. He turned – and gazed all around. "Sheena?" he called. "Sheena? Where *are* you? Sheena?"

No answer.

"Wait!" he screamed at Byron. "My sister! Where is my sister?"

Byron held the mirror steady till the last drip of Monster Blood disappeared into it. "You're not safe here," he said, glancing to the lab door.

"But Sheena—" Billy started.

"Shhh. Listen to me," Byron snapped. "You're in real danger in HorrorLand. I'm not supposed to help you. But I'll try. I'm going to help you escape."

"Escape? I can't escape without Sheena," Billy said.

"Listen to me—" Byron said. "I—"

Before he could finish, two angry-looking Horror MPs – guys we'd never seen before – stepped into the doorway. One of them pulled a slender black club from a holster at his waist. He moved forward quickly, eyes locked on Billy and me. His partner blocked the exit.

I let out a long sigh. No escape this time. We were trapped.

"What did we *do*?" I cried. "Why are you after us?"

"Let's go, Byron," the MP said. He bumped past me and grabbed Byron by the shoulder.

"Don't make a fuss, Byron," the Horror Cop at the doorway called. "Just come along quietly."

I held my breath. What was happening here? They weren't after us? They had come for Byron?

"Let *go* of me!" Byron boomed. He jerked his shoulder free and lurched away from the MP.

The little mirror fell from his hand. It hit the floor and shattered into a dozen pieces.

"Help me!" the Horror Cop yelled to his partner. He grabbed Byron again and held him with both hands.

The other cop dropped to the floor and began frantically picking up mirror pieces.

"Weird!" I let out a cry as I saw what was happening to the mirror.

The jagged pieces on the floor – they were

melting. Turning to liquid under the MP's fingers. They gleamed like little silver puddles.

Grunting to himself, the big MP scooped up the mirror droplets. He climbed to his feet. "Ready to roll," he told his partner.

Byron struggled to free himself from the MP's grasp. "You can't do this!" he insisted. "Don't you know who I am?"

"Shut up and walk," the Horror snapped.

They dragged Byron out of the lab. He screamed and struggled the whole way.

I felt dazed. Too confused to think clearly. I turned to Billy. He looked very upset.

He had trickles of sweat rolling down the sides of his face. And I heard him calling in a soft whisper . . . "Sheena? Are you OK? Sheena? Are you here? Answer me! Please!"

Silence.

Billy wiped the sweat off his cheeks. He spoke in a trembling voice. "She's . . . gone, Matt. Do you think she was sucked into the little mirror, too?"

I shuddered. This was *too weird*.

"We have to go after Byron," I said. "He wanted to help us. That's why they dragged him away. We have to find him. He's the only one who can bring back Sheena."

"But – where?" Billy asked.

Then I spotted something. A tiny piece of silver gleaming at my feet.

I bent down and carefully picked it up. "Billy, look. A piece of the mirror. It didn't melt. That MP didn't get all of the pieces."

Billy pressed close to me. We both stared into the tiny piece of mirror.

"No way!" I shouted. "No way!"

In the tiny triangle of glass, I saw the two missing girls. Britney and Molly.

They were riding on an old-fashioned carousel. With creamy white horses and carriages.

The girls were sitting side by side in a carriage, slowly spinning on the ride.

And the carousel was covered in FLAMES!

To be continued in . . .

Before HorrorLand,
there was

MONSTER BLOOD

Turn the page for a peek at
R.L. Stine's classic prequel.

The substance inside the can was bright green. It shimmered like jelly in the light from the ceiling fixture.

"Touch it," Andy said.

But before Evan had a chance, she reached a finger in and poked it. "It's cold," she said. "Touch it. It's really cold."

Evan poked it with his finger. It was cold, thicker than jelly, heavier.

He pushed his finger beneath the surface. When he pulled his finger out, it made a loud sucking noise.

"Gross," Andy said.

Evan shrugged. "I've seen worse."

"I'll bet it glows in the dark," Andy said, hurrying over to the light switch by the door. "It looks like the green that glows in the dark."

She turned off the ceiling light, but late afternoon sunlight still poured in through the window curtains. "Try the closet," she instructed excitedly.

Evan carried the can into the closet. Andy followed and closed the door. "Yuck. Mothballs," she cried. "I can't breathe."

The Monster Blood definitely glowed in the dark. A circular ray of green light seemed to shine from the can.

"Wow. That's way cool," Andy said, holding her nose to keep out the pungent aroma of the mothballs.

"I've had other stuff that did this," Evan said, more than a little disappointed. "It was called Alien Stuff or Yucky Glop, something like that."

"Well, if you don't want it, I'll take it," Andy replied.

"I didn't say I didn't want it," Evan said quickly.

"Let's get out of here," Andy begged.

Evan pushed open the door and they rushed out of the closet, slamming the door shut behind them. Both of them sucked in fresh air for a few seconds.

"Whew, I hate that smell!" Evan declared. He looked around to see that Andy had taken a handful of Monster Blood from the can.

She squeezed it in her palm. "It feels even colder outside the can," she said, grinning at him. "Look. When you squeeze it flat, it pops right back."

"Yeah. It probably bounces, too," Evan said, unimpressed. "Try bouncing it against the floor. All those things bounce like rubber."

Andy rolled the glob of Monster Blood into a ball and dropped it to the floor. It bounced back up into her hand. She bounced it a little harder. This time it rebounded against the wall and went flying out the bedroom door.

"It bounces really well," she said, chasing it out into the hall. "Let's see if it stretches." She grabbed it with both hands and pulled, stretching it into a long string. "Yep. It stretches, too."

"Big deal," Evan said. "The stuff I had before bounced and stretched really well, too. I thought this stuff was going to be different."

"It stays cold, even after it's been in your hand," Andy said, returning to the room.

Evan glanced at the wall and noticed a dark, round stain by the floorboard. "Uh-oh. Look, Andy. That stuff stains."

"Let's take it outside and toss it around," she suggested.

"OK," he agreed. "We'll go out back. That way, Trigger won't be so lonely."

Evan held out the can, and Andy replaced the ball of Monster Blood. Then they headed downstairs and out to the garden, where they were greeted by Trigger, who acted as if they'd been away for at least twenty years.

The dog finally calmed down and sat in the shade of a tree, panting noisily. "Good boy," Evan said softly. "Take it easy. Take it easy, old fella."

Andy reached into the can and pulled out a green glob. Then Evan did the same. They rolled the stuff in their hands until they had two ball-shaped globs. Then they began to play catch with them.

"It's amazing how they don't lose their shape," Andy said, tossing a green ball high in the air.

Evan shielded his eyes from the late afternoon sun and caught the ball with one hand. "All this stuff is the same," he said. "It isn't so special."

"Well, I think it's cool," Andy said defensively.

Evan's next toss was too high. The green ball of gunk sailed over Andy's outstretched hands.

"Whoa!" Andy called.

"Sorry," Evan called.

They both stared as the ball bounced once, twice, then landed right in front of Trigger.

Startled, the dog jumped to his feet and lowered his nose to sniff it.

"No, boy!" Evan called. "Leave it alone. Leave it alone, boy!"

As disobedient as ever, Trigger lowered his head and licked the glowing green ball.

"No, boy! Drop! Drop!" Evan called, alarmed.

He and Andy both lunged towards the dog.

But they were too slow.

Trigger picked up the ball of Monster Blood in his teeth and began chewing it.

"No, Trigger!" Evan shouted. "Don't swallow it. Don't swallow!"

Trigger swallowed it.

"Oh, no!" Andy cried, balling her hands into fists at her sides. "Now there isn't enough left for us to share!"

But that wasn't what was troubling Evan. He bent down and prised apart the dog's jaws. The green blob was gone. Swallowed.

"Stupid dog," Evan said softly, releasing the dog's mouth.

He shook his head as troubling thoughts poured into his mind.

What if the stuff makes Trigger ill? Evan wondered.

What if the stuff is poison?

About the Author

R.L. Stine's books are read all over the world. So far, his books have sold more than 300 million copies, making him one of the most popular children's authors in history. Besides Goosebumps, R.L. Stine has written the teen series Fear Street and the funny series Rotten School, as well as the Mostly Ghostly series, The Nightmare Room series, and the two-book thriller *Dangerous Girls*. R.L. Stine lives in New York with his wife, Jane, and Minnie, his King Charles spaniel. You can learn more about him at www.RLStine.com.

FEAR
FILE
#3

WELCOME TO
HORRORLAND
WHERE NIGHTMARES COME TO LIFE!
HorrorLand is
NOT what it
used to be!

Working Hard
to Keep You Unsafe!
SUPPORT
YOUR
MONSTER
POLICE
IF YOU NEED US, JUST SCREAM.
A CRY FOR HELP IS MUSIC TO OUR FIVE EARS!
A Special
8-Fingered
Salute to...
MP OFFICER OF THE MONTH:
Howard U. Likapunchindanose
Unlikeable · Unhelpful · Untrustworthy · Unspeakable
HOWARD HAS A SPECIAL HEARTFELT MESSAGE FOR HORRORLAND VISITORS:
"DON'T START ANYTHING.
YOU KNOW HOW I GET."
FIND THE REST at
WWW.ESCAPEHorrorLAND.COM
SIGNED,
LM1
HorrorLand
www.EnterHorrorLand.com

MAP
#3
POLICE